YOU CANNOT Imprison AN EAGLE'S DREAM

 W9-CXY-954

ALBA ERA

outskirts
press

You Cannot Imprison an Eagle's Dream
All Rights Reserved.
Copyright © 2018 Alba Era
v3.0

The opinions expressed in this manuscript are solely the opinions of the author and do not represent the opinions or thoughts of the publisher. The author has represented and warranted full ownership and/or legal right to publish all the materials in this book.

This book may not be reproduced, transmitted, or stored in whole or in part by any means, including graphic, electronic, or mechanical without the express written consent of the publisher except in the case of brief quotations embodied in critical articles and reviews.

Outskirts Press, Inc.
http://www.outskirtspress.com

ISBN: 978-1-4787-9255-0

Library of Congress Control Number: 2017916330

Cover Photo © 2018 Outskirts Press, Inc. All rights reserved - used with permission.

Outskirts Press and the "OP" logo are trademarks belonging to Outskirts Press, Inc.

PRINTED IN THE UNITED STATES OF AMERICA

Quotation from the book :

"I will kill you and the horse! yelled he wildly again.

Come on! Heave-ho! was he calling, screaming and whipping the poor animal. Move forward, you dirty animal! And kept hitting the horse wildly and brutally. I was feeling like each whip on the horse's body was hitting me, too. Tears were running down from the big eyes of the horse. And it seemed to me that his tears and mine had the same rhythm.

- Don't, please! I called out loudly stretching my hands to the horse. But he ignored my call and continued :

- Come on! Go ahead! I don't feed you for no reason, you dirty animal! Walk ahead! Walk! And the whip kept flying up and hissing in the air, leaving swollen lines on the horse's back.

Oh! How much hatred I felt at that moment! I really pitied the poor horse. He, my husband, was using the horse to kill me! But the horse seemed as if he had understood his goal and stood still not moving an inch. And me, already frozen like a statue, was only two feet away from the horse."......

Prologue

Dear reader,

Do you know that in our modern times, in some small countries, and particularly in those of the Eastern World, violence against women is still being practiced? The dreams of young girls continue to be suppressed, and all this in the name of the inherited tradition. This phenomenon has been fought and continues to be fought by democratic youth all over the world, including the Western World. But, here and there, there still are zealous inheritors who try to preserve this ancient yet inhuman tradition. We all like the positive inherited traditions that serve the stability and permanence of the family, but we must instill respect for the family and to everybody in general. It is dead wrong that the dreams of many, many young girls today are being suppressed. To this tradition we have to say No....

Is there actually female suppression in our world today, you ask?

Yes, really, dear reader, there are still such countries where girls are engaged in their early childhood, and their families and relatives choose their future husbands.. In our day, unfortunately, there are still such stories similar to that of the girl that this author describes. Although she was only sixteen, her dreams and desires were senselessly cut off. With a crushed heart, she had no choice but to accept her fate determined by this inherited tradition.

Only when she could endure no longer; when she understood that she had the right to dream beautiful dreams, only then, at last she made the right decision to say stop to the violence and fight for her deserved freedom.

Violence, anywhere and on anybody, has one, and only one verdict::
It must be stopped!

*Part
One*

You Cannot Imprison an Eagle's Dream

I was only fifteen years old when everything seemed under my control. Up to those moments my life had been quiet and almost without raw emotion. Most of the time my parents used to work hard simply to make sure that I, my four sisters and our brother, had enough food, clothing and shelter. Next thing they did very well was to give us an education based on love and respect for all children in the family. Though nonsensical childish quarrels often took place among us siblings, still, when it came to serious problems that any of us might have, we all would unite and even shed tears for one another. Our father was rather quiet, loving and tolerant. Our mother was a bit tougher and strict. She always used to tell us, "Do not make me feel ashamed of you! I want to always hold my head up and be proud of you."

In 1982 many marriages in my country were still arranged through family matchmaking. Parents would consider it a shame if their daughter had a boyfriend. And it was considered an honor when girls listened and allowed their parents to choose their husbands. Usually girls had to marry before age twenty. If a girl reached twenty-five and was still not married, she would be considered too old or second hand.

When I was in high school I had my dreams and desires as any other 15-year-old girl. I was proud of my family that sacrificed to send me to one of the best schools. I also felt proud of myself. I was 5.6 feet, with dark brown colored skin, and had long and curly hair. My eyes were big and brown and very expressive. My eyebrows were uniquely beautiful, and, when looking in the mirror, I used to say: even a painter could not have designed them more beautifully than that. At school, besides learning, I played sports like basketball, I danced, wrote poems or read interesting books for my age. I loved my teachers, though they were strict, and I was curious enough to ask them about anything I wanted to know and learn.

There were twenty-eight students in my class and I started to make friends with all of them very easily. I realized that I was growing fast when I noticed that my body was taking another shape and my breasts would not hide anymore under my loose blouse. So were my buttocks looking somehow prominent on my long thin body.

I had two very close girlfriends in my class. And it was not that I did not like boys, but at that time it was a taboo to have a friend with whom to share your daily life problems or feelings. Still, now and then, I broke that taboo by going to a particular boy's desk. His name was Arbi. He had a kind of smile that gave you a special feeling for him. And I noticed that he would smile whenever I went close to him. One of my closest friends, named Lili, once told me, "I think Arbi likes you."

"No," I said. "He smiles at all of us like that." Even my other best friend, Dita, added,

"He never smiles at me, though I live in the same neighborhood with him."

Dita was dark-haired and Lili was blonde. Dita was a better organized girl and a better listener, who did her homework every day. Lili was the beauty of the class, but not well-organized. I loved both of them with all my heart.

Days were passing fast and the end of our school year arrived. Two weeks before the summer holidays a contagious disease spread in our school, and all of us had to be examined and tested. It was Hepatitis B virus–jaundice. Two days after the test they sent me to the hospital to be isolated. I felt completely alone. My boy- and girlfriends could only see me through the window. Arbi visited me more often and we stood for hours on end communicating with signs through the window glass. Nobody was allowed to come inside because of the contagious disease. Inside the hospital you could see strange faces, sometimes even scary. Many were children, and I would often go to their room. A little boy, named Mario was always crying more than the others. He was only three years old. One day I took him into my arms, cleaned his face, wiped the tears running down from his big eyes, and walked him back and forth in the hospital corridor.

"Why are you crying, Mario?" I asked him. "We are going to play together; don't cry, please!"

-"No," he said, "I want my mother."

"It's okay," I said. "Mom is coming soon."

Actually I was feeling so sad for him that tears ran down my face, though I tried to stop. Strangely enough, he stopped crying and asked me, "Why are you crying?"

"I want my mom, too," I said, "but the doctor won't let me see her before I get healed. I can only see her from inside my window. You may also come to this window and do the same."

"Yes," he said, with a sweet smile only possible with children of his age. I smiled, too, and hugged him, and told him that now we were friends. He was feeling tired and I put him in his bed, and kissed him lightly on his forehead before he fell asleep. I stood looking at him and wondered: how is it possible that a three-year-old child brought me for a few minutes into a very simple and uncomplicated world?! At that moment I wished I were three again. But all these thoughts were suddenly interrupted by some steps behind me. A shadow was approaching closer to me and I heard a voice from behind, "What's up?"

I turned around, somehow scared.

"Nothing," I said. "Who are you?"

"I am a patient in this hospital. My name is Jon." His head was almost shaved, and his thick, black eyebrows made him a scary spectre.

"Are you related to Mario?" he asked.

"No," I said, "just felt sorry for him; –he's such a very little child.

"So do I," he added.

I had to turn my head away from him to avoid his persistent stare.

"What's your name?" he asked me.

Quickly, I ran away very scared. How could I tell my name to a stranger? While running through the hospital corridor, I heard him say from behind me, "I will find out your name! You have nowhere to go!"

I quickly closed the door of my room. Then I went to the window to see if there were any other visitors outside. But no one was there. The world outside seemed as lonely as it was inside the hospital. That moment my thoughts were interrupted by the doctor, who came in and asked:

"How are you, little girl?" His strong voice gave him a sense of authority.

"I am feeling well. When am I going to leave the hospital, doctor?"

"Just be patient. Everything is going well. Your blood tests show better this time. I think you are going to leave in a few days."

This news made me happy. Just after that I heard a knock on the window and turned my head, surprised. Both my parents were behind the window pane.

"Mom and Dad, soon I am leaving the hospital," I said cheerfully.

"We know it," they said. "We just spoke with the doctor. Your sisters are eagerly waiting for you to come home. They miss you so much."

"I miss them," I said. "It is like a prison here. Have you brought me something good to eat?"

"Yes," answered my mom, "pancakes and fresh yoghurt."

"Your mother made them this morning for you," added my father.

I really enjoyed that delicious food. After a while I was feeling tired and fell into a deep sleep. I saw a very strange dream. I was in a field of flowers, running happily all around, breathing in the clean air together with the aroma of flowers. When I opened my eyes, I felt bad, realizing it was unreal. Still, that night seemed short to me because of the thought that I was leaving the hospital soon and the second grade high school year would start in a few days. I was eagerly waiting to see my classmates again. I kept wondering what they might have done during summer holidays.

The day came to leave the hospital. The rules were that, before leaving, you should return all stuff you had used, like towels, sheets, glasses, etc. By accident I had broken a glass and went to the nurse to inform her about it.

"I am sorry to disturb you, but one glass was broken. What am I supposed to do?" Two nurses heard me and looked at each other.

"You have to pay for it, that is all," spoke one of them, who had big eyes, long hair and a hat on her head. The other was blonde and, strangely enough, had black eyes.

"Okay," I said in a low voice.

On my way out of nurse's room, quite suddenly I saw the same scary man with flat-cut hair. This made me think that he was following me everywhere. I ran quickly away and straight to my room. Before I could close the door, he put his foot out to block it.

"What's the news?" he repeated.

"What do you want from me?" I said to him, this time in a more decisive voice.

"Nothing," he answered. "I heard that you are leaving the hospital, and I am glad for that."

"Can you please remove your foot because I'm tired and want to sleep."

"You are a beautiful girl. I like you. What do you think about..." But before he finished, I forced the door closed and locked it from inside.

"I told you that you have nowhere to go. I will find you wherever you may be!"

"Away with you!" I dared say it to him in a secure tone, knowing that the door was locked from inside.

Next day the doctor examined me and said that everything looked okay, and I could go home. I turned in all the hospital stuff and figured I'd take the urban bus and go straight home just to surprise my family. In a few hours I arrived home, a bit tired. My parents were happy, but surprised, too. "You have grown so much," my mom told me. "Your breasts looks bigger now. Try to cover them with big loose blouses. In a few days you are going to start school and we have to buy you some new clothes."

The days I spent with my family were really enjoyable. And I played a lot with the cousins of my age. However, one day my big cousin called and said, "You girls are grown ups now, go inside! Don't you see that you are already big enough to get married?"

"But you know what?" I interrupted, "you better marry yourself first, before you tell this to us!" After saying that I ran into the house as I knew what I might expect from him.

The day of school came. I had to travel to the school in town. I took my suitcase with a few clothes, hugged all family members and, before leaving, told them:

"I don't know when I may come back; please come and see me

some time." I had tears in my eyes, knowing that my school was far away from my village.

In school I slept in a big dorm room together with eighteen other girls. We had bunk beds, just like in the army barracks. The first day I met all my roommate friends. Each one of them had changed a lot. They all told their stories how and where they had passed their holidays. I was so eager to go back to the classroom and meet all my classmates. Half of them did not live in the dorm as their homes were close to the school. I was especially thinking about one of my classmates - Arbi. He had visited me quite often in the hospital and each time had given me his special smile.

"You always keep your mouth open and I can see your teeth," I joked once with him.

"It's my smile," he answered, "I do it only with you."

He was tall and had dark brown hair. I wouldn't say he was very handsome, but very attractive, and had a solid muscular body. One late evening, when alone and thinking about him, I felt some kind of burning in my body. What are these thoughts about him? I wondered, and then tried to forget by closing my eyes in an attempt to sleep. Morning came soon. I heard the guardian of the dorm calling to other rooms to wake up.

"Get up girls, It's time to come out!"

I dressed quickly, combed my hair and looked at myself carefully in the mirror. I felt like something was missing. Maybe I would tie my hair up and make a pigtail. That way I may feel more comfortable.

"Hurry up!" Eli told me. "Will you have breakfast or not?"

I did not answer. Eli was from my village, too. She was a bit fat for her age, but very well-educated.

"Ema!" I heard her voice again. "Come on, now! Why four hours in front of the mirror?"

"Coming," I said. I took my school bag with a few books and notebooks in it, and ran to the line in front of the dorm waiting to have breakfast.

I sat at the table with my girlfriends. We had butter, jam and a little bread, which I always enjoyed. I drank a cup of tea and ran quickly straight to my classroom. It was only a five minute walk to my school. As soon as I stepped in, I heard voices.

"Oh, God! How much you have changed!" It was my friends, Lili and Dita. We hugged each other, talking loudly. Then I met all the other girl- and boyfriends of the class. Quickly I glanced around the room, but did not see Arbi yet.

"Dita! Where is he?" I spoke in a low voice.

"He was here only five minutes ago. Why? Have you missed him?" she asked with an ironic smile on her lips.

"Like all the other girls," I said, feeling somehow ashamed.

"There he is," said Dita. At that time Arbi was hugging everybody. I was almost at the back of the class. While looking at him, I dropped my pen and was trying to pick it up. Before I straightened up, I felt someone bending just in front of my face. I looked up. It was Arbi.

"Arbi!" I said in a hoarse voice.

"I found you at last!" he said with his smile which seemed never-ending. He hugged me the same as others and whispered in my ear:

"I have missed you so much!"

Then we stopped hugging, still holding our hands tight. Before thinking further, I embraced him again, and spoke something to him, "Me, too." Within me I felt that strange burning in my stomach.

"What is it? You look red like a tomato!" said Arbi in a soft, warm voice.

"Nothing," I said. "What color should I have?"

"We'll talk later, okay?" said Arbi with the same warm voice which seemed to penetrate deep into my heart. But our teacher's steps interrupted us.

"Good day to everybody! Are you all well?" the teacher said.

"Very well!" said most of us.

"Okay. Today, being the first day of school, your schedule will be rather reduced, which means the day will be shorter."

While listening to the teacher talking, I turned my head to the bench on my right side where Arbi was sitting. Feeling me watching him, he turned his head, too, and we crossed our eyes. Feeling somehow shy after his persistent look, and thinking that he had seen me looking at him, I bent my head down and acted as if I was writing something. The first day of school was over. The heavy sound of the school bell echoing through the corridors put all students on the move and you could hear classmates greeting one another. We'll see you tomorrow, was their common wish.

"Have a good afternoon!" said Dita. I did the same and gave her a smile.

"Goodbye! We'll see you tomorrow," I said to my other close friend, Lili.

"Okay," said Lili, throwing her school bag on her shoulder. Her blonde curly hair flowed down her back. She was very beautiful. And I was proud to have her as a close friend, though she did not excel at lessons. Before leaving, she came to hug me, and said, "I have a lot of things to talk about with you. Maybe I will come one day to the dorm and tell you everything."

"Come this Saturday, if you want."

"Perhaps I may," said Lili and ran out of school.

I had not left the classroom yet. Arbi, on the other side of the class, had not moved either. I pretended as if I was getting ready to go out.

"Wait," said Arbi. "Don't leave, please!"

I sat feeling happy to have the chance to stay a while with him. We spoke for a while about everything we had done during the holidays. After a silent moment, I heard Arbi's voice again:

"How do you feel now?"

"I'm feeling good after the long treatment in the hospital."

"Oh, no. I'm asking you how you are feeling being here with me." His eyes were looking straight into mine. The same strange feeling went through my body. I felt my heart beating fast. His hand went up in the air and touched the bangs over my forehead. His fingers touched my face.

"You have become very beautiful," he said in a voice that seemed to lose strength. "Please, talk to me! Tell me something!"

I continued to look at him, lost in an incomprehensible world, and extremely pleased being with him.

"I don't know what to tell," I murmured and was scared at the idea that this lovely moment would end soon. "We are in the same class," I said, "and we are close friends. That's all I can say." After this I took a deep breath, feeling as if I had said my piece.

"It is true," he said. "But don't you think that there is something more between us? Don't you understand that I like to stay near you?"

"Shush…" I said, trying to stop him, scared that I might hear something I couldn't handle at that moment. Unintentionally I tapped his lips with my finger. He kissed it lightly. His hands grabbed mine. His face was now very close to mine. I could feel his breath from half-opened lips. Oh! How eagerly I wanted to kiss him right there! Right at that moment! A hundred thoughts were blowing my mind! Yes, no, yes, no. A very light movement from Arbi and I closed my eyes. Our lips were tight together for a long time, followed by many more wet kisses. It was the inner electricity that made our kisses so powerful. I felt his strong hands holding my waist fast and tight. I just moved a little away from his body, feeling I was almost flying to the sky. I tried to speak but was not sure what to say. Maybe I was whispering something. Arbi was smiling.

"Do you know what the date is today?"

"Yes," I said, "the third of September."

Arbi took something out of his pocket and started to write on his bench: "Sept. 3. First kiss. Arbi and Ema." Then looked at me happily, and added:

"Millions of kisses will come after this." He laughed loudly and kissed me again. I kissed him back with passion. We kissed and kissed again and again. A long time had elapsed. An absolute serenity was all around us.

"We better go now," I said, using a decisive tone. Arbi looked at me in the eye and said, "Okay. Let's go!" And we walked hand in hand through the long corridor of the school. I wished that corridor would never end. Arbi kept squeezing my hand repeatedly as if to tell me that he was feeling the same. "Well, we're at the main exit door," said Arbi.

"Where are you going now?" I asked with a pang of regret that we had to separate. He smiled and said, "I will wait here until you go inside the dorm and come out at the window to give me a last kiss. After that I will go home."

Arbi's face had actually turned red. And maybe mine was too.

"We'll see you tomorrow morning," I told him and walked away with unstable steps unwilling to leave. When inside, I ran to my room on the third floor and straight to the window. Arbi was sitting on the pavement. I made a sign of a kiss to him with my hand. He responded with a gesture as if catching my kiss in the air and he brought his hand to his heart. At that moment I had an idea. I gave him a signal not to go away yet, and grabbed a piece of paper where I wrote: " You're my dearest spirit." I wrapped it up, threw it to him and waited at the window until he got it and opened it. I saw him put both hands on his chest, a simple symbol to tell me that I was there in his heart. I returned to my room and threw myself on the bed. My cheeks were still burning.

"What is it with you?" asked Eli. "You did not come to eat lunch either!"

"I am not hungry," I said, and pretended to fluff my pillow, to avoid her gaze. Then she came closer to me with something in hand.

"I brought your lunch. Here, eat it later when you are hungry."

I thanked her and got lost in my thoughts again. I kept recalling everything that happened and smiled happily just like an idiot.

"Ooooh, someone has fallen in love!" It was my roommate. Some other girls accompanied her, laughing or repeating the long ooooh-s.

"You better shut up!" I warned them, though inside myself I was actually liking the teases.

Next morning I got up early and was more careful and better organized in everything. I even stared more often in the mirror. I ate breakfast and ran to the classroom. When I entered the room, Dita threw a strange look at me.

"What?" I asked her. She was a neighbor to Arbi. While coming to school Arbi had told her everything.

I had already sensed that such a thing might happen.

"What is it you know?" I asked her, feeling that my face had become red again.

"Both of you - you and Arbi...." At that moment Lili entered the room and heard Dita saying, ...You and Arbi....

"Exactly what happened?" she asked very curiously.

"Read here!" said Dita, pointing with her finger at Arbi's bench.

"Oh, God! When so?"

"Yesterday after school," I said happily and proudly.

The three of us jumped up in the air, embracing one another.

"What's going on here?" asked Arbi the moment he entered the classroom.

"Listen, Arbi! The whole class knew about this. The way you looked at each other, or how you cared for each other, one could easily understand that you two were in love. And I am so pleased that you said it openly at last." Lili gave Arbi a high five.

So the whole class knew now about our feelings. Days went by without much notice. I was very glad, but scared, too. If my parents learned that I had a boyfriend, they would take me away from school. This I discussed with Arbi, as well.

Don't worry!" he told me. "We are going to keep it secret until we finish school." I liked Arbi's idea.

"You talk to Eli about it, too! She is from your village."

And I did so before we slept. "Please, Eli, be careful not to speak to anybody in the village about this."

She promised, and, laughing, asked me to do her a favor:

"You help me in language and literacy, as I hate those compositions they ask us to write."

"That's very easy. Each time we have to write compositions, I will write two - one for you, one for me."

After this we continued to tell private jokes until we fell asleep.

In the morning we lined up in front of the school and the school principal delivered a speech. I didn't know, but it seemed that something had happened in school because all teachers looked concerned. His speech was long, but I was not able to understand the purpose of that speech. In the end I heard that our state leader had died. The principal asked us to have one minute of silence. After that the whole school sang the national anthem. Then we were told that we had to complete a two-week military training. Several instructions were given about this. Each morning we had to line up dressed in military uniform and go up the hills around the city to do the military training. To me those two weeks of training were the most beautiful time in my life. We did not have to prepare any lessons and I didn't even understand the policy regarding why we had to do this training. The only thing to do was to practice hitting the target. Actually I did not care at all about the training. I just stayed near my friends with pencil in hand and took notes about what the training officer was saying.

Arbi was always by my side in the next line. I was very careful with the signs I made to him so the teacher wouldn't know how we felt about each other. Time and again Arbi would repeat clicking his pen as a signal for me to turn my head. I used to smile back to him. At noon they left us free for two hours and we got together, making jokes and playing different games. Most of the time I would stay near Arbi, always careful not to be noticed by others.

I still remember one of the training days in particular. It was a nice

May day. All the girls had gotten together during the free time. Lili was telling us how she'd met a very handsome boy.

"He lived very near my home," she said. "It was strange how I had not seen him before."

"Because you weren't even able to blow and clean your nose," interrupted Dita. All of us burst into laughter.

"I don't know whether my parents would allow me to see and get to know him," said Lili, this time seriously.

I was thinking whether only we, the girls in the village, had these problems. Everywhere seemed to be the same. Our parents did not understand that the arranged marriage was old fashioned now.

"You know what happened to me the first week?" continued Lili. "My parents brought someone to our home and wanted me to be engaged with him. I told my mom, 'May be you marry him, but not me'."

Lili continued to quote her mother, "You make my life miserable my daughter. You don't have to be the first to change the laws."

"Why not?" intervened Dita, using a strong voice. "Why shouldn't we be the first to make the revolution?"

I liked Dita's view. Her words gave me some courage. At this moment one of the girls called out, "Hey girls, girls! Why don't we decide all together here that we never marry anymore through matchmaking?"

Most of the girls joined their voices and their hands in agreement with this idea. My heart was beating heavily in my chest. I felt as if I was in a time of war I'd heard described by my father, except for one difference: at the time of Second World War the enemy was straight in front of you. But now our war was much more difficult. We had to fight against our parents, against their backward customs and traditions without hurting their hearts. And I don't know why I had so many emotions. I had tears in my eyes. I didn't know if I would dare and be so strong as to tell my parents that I would not marry the person they had chosen for me.

Among all these emotions, while all of us girls were so joyous, the voice of Natasha, one of the girls in the class, was heard saying:

"You girls today are out of balance, indeed. If I dare say 'no' to my father, he will kill me." After this we all got lost in thoughts.

Finally I said, "I know, but we have to try at least."

Suddenly all this talk and noise was interrupted by Arbi, who walked up next to me with a bunch of flowers in his hand. Lili was the first to turn her head.

- "Flowers for me? How sweet!" All the girls laughed loudly.

"Come on, Lili!" said Arbi. "You may take just one flower from the bunch. I have for thirty minutes wandered around waiting to pick them up. I want my beloved friend to keep these flowers in her hands."

Though shy for the moment because of that lovely open gesture Arbi made, I received the flowers, and, with my cheeks red, thanked him for the gift.

"Just a thanks?" asked Arbi with the smile on his face.

"Ooooh! He wants a kiss," said the girls teasingly. Then many of them left just to give us some time alone.

"Why are you staying that far from me? Come closer!"

When I saw that girls had left, I threw my hands around Arbi's neck, giving him several kisses, and asked him, "How do you know that I love flowers?"

"Because I thought, mmm... she looks like a flower, she smells like a flower. She must love flowers. You are my flower!"

Then he came closer to me, and, a little more serious, said, "Today you look more beautiful." Then he looked straight into my eyes, and touched my lips, which that moment were burning for a kiss. His fingers brushed my face. Feeling his touch I closed my eyes, and my heart beat faster and faster. My whole body felt like flying into another world. It was a lovely and strange feeling! His fingers stopped at my chin.

"Hold your head up, and look into my eyes!" said Arbi. I saw him somehow scared. I don't know what it was, but sometimes I could not look at him for a long time. I wanted to embrace him, to kiss, and kiss him endlessly.

"What?" I asked, in my own lost world for a moment.

"I have not heard yet from your mouth the word that our hearts say almost every day! Feel no shyness!" he said. A long kiss on Arbi's lips said everything. His eyes were fixed on me. "Ema, I love you much… much! I am the happiest man in the world! What about you? How do you feel?" he asked me, somehow relaxed after having said what he felt.

"Arbi," I started to speak, holding his hands tightly, not knowing why.

"And I love you, too!"

"What? I didn't hear you well," he said with a huge smile.

"I love you so much!"

Silence prevailed for a moment, our eyes locked in an embrace. I looked down at nowhere, waiting for Arbi to say something. When I looked up again to see his eyes, tears were running down his face.

"Do not worry," he said. "They are tears of joy. Then we embraced each other and stayed like that for a while in each other's arms. After a few minutes we saw that all the others were staying in line for the last call.

"We have to go," said Arbi, following this with a light kiss on my forehead.

God! How warm and loving was that kiss! How much security and strength it gave me!

"Let's go." I had to say it though sad that we had to separate.

"Don't feel sad, we'll see each other every day! I am not going home without giving you my goodnight kiss for today!"

Arbi's words made me feel better. That day had passed very fast. I went to join the long line of students in military uniform. And I am not sure whether I was thinking or speaking aloud, because I heard Lili say:

"Yes, it is true."

I couldn't truly believe the decision that many of us girls had voiced. It was a great and momentous thing that we'd decided not to marry through matchmaking.

"And, you know what?" I told Lili, "this Saturday I will go home. It is three weeks now that I have not seen my family. I do miss them, but I don't know if they will give me permission for that. She was listening very attentively and asked me:

"Why do you need permission to go to your family?"

"Yes, all the girls who live in the school dormitory must have a strong reason to go home."

- "And what will be your reason?" asked Dita, standing behind me.

"Because I miss my family.

"Good reason, indeed. Better tell them the truth."

We'll see tomorrow, were the words by many of the girls and boys of our class. Only six girls from our class lived in the dorm.

"Let's go and have lunch before they close the kitchen," said Miranda, one of the six.

"You go first! I'll catch you in a few minutes." I ran up the steps of the dorm and started singing as soon as I entered my room. I threw my school bag on the bed and went to the window to see Arbi, who, as always, was sitting there. He saw me and asked:

"Are you alone?"

"Yes," I said.

"I heard that you will go home. May I accompany you?"

"No, no way! What if someone whom we know sees us? How would I explain that to my parents?"

"Well then, only up to the bus station?"

"That makes a difference," I said relaxing.

"That's good. See you tomorrow!"

As usual, I sent him my kiss through the air. He did the same gesture catching my kiss in the air and putting his hand on his chest. Happy, I let Arbi go, and walked down the long corridor until I found myself in the dining room. All the girls had already finished eating and I saw my plate with some pasta and a piece of sausage on top. I ate it quickly.

"Careful, you are almost choking!" spoke somebody in front of me. Feeling somehow ashamed, I slowed down. He was a boy from the other class. I was wondering why he came to our eating table. When upstairs, I asked Eli, "What did he want at our table?"

"I don't know," she answered, "but it's obvious that he likes one of our girls."

Rita, one of our girls, had become red-faced.

"He is crazy," said Rita.

"What about you, Rita? How do you feel?" I asked her with a smile. We all laughed together.

"Listen, girls. Do not take it seriously! He has not told me anything at all," answered Rita. "He just speaks to me here and there, like good morning, good evening, what's up, as if he doesn't know what else to say."

I put the military hat on my head and tried to play the role of that boy. I came close to Rita and said:

"What's up, Rita? I like you very much, please give me a kiss!"

All the girls burst out laughing loudly. Rita didn't care about what I said. She took the pillow nearby and hit me with it. Then she added, "Your mind thinks of nothing else but Arbi. But I have come here to learn and not play amorous games."

"Yes, yes, we are going to see about that," I said, and after that I left her alone.

Saturday came. I got up and stood in line to take a bath. Most of the girls were still sleeping, so I did not have to wait long in line. I took the bath, got ready and went down to ask the principal of the dorm for permission to go home. He was a good-natured person, but very somber.

"Excuse me, Mr. Principal, may I ask you something?"

"One minute," he said, without raising his head from his desk. Then he asked: "What do you want?"

"I need permission to go home. It is over three weeks now that I have not seen my family."

"What is your name?"

I told him my full name in a confident voice.

"Here is your permission. You have to be back tomorrow before four o'clock p. m., okay?"

I was so happy to get the permission. Grabbed my suitcase, already packed, and ran straight to the bus station, where I should meet Arbi. I looked around but did not see him anywhere yet. I jumped into the bus rather worried.

"Ready everyone?" said the driver. "We'll depart in two minutes. Just take your seats. The door was closing when I saw a hand pushing the door open and somebody jumped into the bus. It was Arbi.

"Where were you?" I asked him quickly.

"In the store. Bought something for your family. Just tell them that you have bought it." I looked straight in his eyes with a happy feeling.

"Why do you have to think about everything?" I asked him.

"Because I love you so much, my flower!"

"Don't raise your voice, others can hear us." My voice surprised him.

"Listen," he said, "we are growing older now, and eventually we must let others know that we love each other, okay?"

Most of the passengers in the bus were young. I wasn't feeling ashamed of others, but among them I saw someone my parents' age looking at me suspiciously. I was only sixteen then, sitting next to a boy.

The way he and a few others were looking at me made me feel as if they were saying, 'Shame on you!' However, I tried to avoid their gaze. Now and then Arbi would squeeze my hand.

"I am here," he said. "Why do you look through the window?"

"I am very scared," I said, keeping my eyes down. "What if my parents learn about this, how am I going to explain it to them?"

"Tell the truth. You actually have the best grades in lessons. I am quite sure they will feel proud of you."

His words somehow seemed to encourage me. I smiled and relaxed. "You're right."

The trip lasted thirty minutes. I went home and Arbi took the same bus back home.

"Tomorrow I will be waiting for you at the station. I love you much, okay?" said Arbi.

"I love you, too," I said and stepped out of the bus.

Here was my beautiful village and the endless fields around. Small houses were built so close to each other they appeared to be just one long house when seen from afar. Each time I returned to my village, a strange feeling would overwhelm my whole body. It was the love I had for my family, for my home, and everything else around there.

While walking through the narrow alley to the village I felt the steps of somebody behind me. Should I turn my head and see? Better not. Steps were tapping a faster rhythm. My heartbeat was doing the same. Who might it be? Why were those steps running fast? To reach me? I plucked up the courage and turned my head. Oh God! It was that strange person I had seen in hospital! His thick eyebrows reminded me of the same scary person. Still, I thought for a moment: Why should I be afraid? Now I am in my village.

"Why do you follow me?" But my strong voice did not scare him at all.

"Please, listen to me for a moment! Only five minutes, okay?"

"Speak," I said, and kept walking.

"I have seen you everywhere and I like you so much; I want to marry you."

The fear I had toward that man was turned into courage to speak out.

"Listen here!" I said. "First you continue to chase me like a shadow. This is not normal at all. Secondly, I am not interested at all whether you like me or not. I am in love with somebody else. Therefore do not waste time chasing me. Just turn back to where you came from!"

"Oooh! You look even more beautiful when angry!" he said with a cunning look.

"Listen to me. As soon as I go home, I will tell all my cousins to beat you to death."

"Okay, okay, just slow down! Are you trying to frighten me?" He spoke with the same cunning look, which gave me the feeling of disgust.

"I will send people to your house," he continued, "and ask for you to marry me."

Very scared, I spoke in a tough voice:

"You cannot do that because, first of all, you have not got my approval."

Still the tone of my voice made him laugh again.

"It doesn't matter. You will like me later after we get married."

In shock and frightened, I hurried to my house. I didn't dare turn my head around to see him again. Having left that strange man far behind, as soon as I saw the door of my house, I felt completely relieved.

"Ema is here, Ema!"

The voice of my only brother made all the family come out of the house. We hugged in rounds and asked about one another's health.

"Why is your face so red?" asked my mother in a concerned voice.

"I don't know, maybe due to the long walk."

"I know, walking that street is tiring," said my mother and added:

"Let me prepare something for you to eat first. I am sure you are hungry."

"No mother, I am not hungry at all."

"I have cooked some white beans with hot pepper."

"I only need a shower and some sleep, please."

- "Tonight you are not going to sleep. Your elder sister with her husband and the little baby are coming."

"Okay, Mom, but I need to have some rest."

"Yes, go and take a shower! I am sure you will feel better after that."

While taking the shower I was wondering:

Whom could I tell that I had fallen in love? I wouldn't even dare think that I could tell such a thing to my parents. I knew they would never understand me. But yes, maybe I could speak to my elder sister. At least, this was what I was thinking for the moment. And then these thoughts brought me back to Arbi. What was he doing at this very moment? I wished I had him with me....

"Shall I brush your hair?" It was the voice of my sister, **Adriana,** standing behind me. I had to pull myself together.

"Okay," I said.

"Tell me, what is going on at your school?"

"What do you want to know, my dear sister?"

"Everything, dear sister, everything."

I started to talk about teachers, boy- and girlfriends at school, about the noisy town, and.... actually I wanted to tell everything to my sisters, but they were still small.

"I want to marry in the city," said the other sister, younger than Adriana.

"You grow up first," said our mother. Everyone laughed. I felt that our parents were looking at us happily.

"Our girls are almost grown now," said father.

"I know," said mother. "Troubles grow with them, too. People are now knocking at our door asking for our daughters. All this talk was interrupted by a knock on the door. It was our elder sister with her husband, and we made a place for them to sit. All the attention was directed to the little baby. After dinner my elder sister came close to me and said:

"You look quite grown now. Look how big your breasts have become!"

"You'd better look at yours," I said rather quickly.

"Any boy teasing you?"

"No," I said, "but I have a close friend. His name is Arbi…" I continued to talk about him passionately.

"You better stop talking about him now. If father hears these things, he will not let you go to school anymore."

"I know, I know, but I will keep it a secret until I finish school."

"Any other news? How is your progress in school?"

"I am doing well with my lessons."

"Anything else?"

I thought for a moment and added:

"There is someone, somehow crazy, who follows me everywhere."

"Maybe he likes you," my sister said.

"Who cares? Next time if he appears again in front of me, I am going to hit him with a stone straight on his head."

My little sisters laughed again. After that, being pleased with my family, but tired, I went straight to bed.

On Sunday our mother rose early and we could smell the fragrance of the warm pancakes that filled the whole house.

"Mom, don't serve all the pancakes; spare some for my girlfriends at school, please."

"Okay," said Mom. "I will make some more for your friends."

It was eight o'clock in the morning when the elder sister said, "Mom, Mom, some people are at the door!"

"Who might they be?" wondered father, looking through the window.

"I don't know these faces. You better go out and ask them," said Mom. Father went out, clearing his voice:

"Hi, how are you, and who are you?" asked Father.

"We are some friends."

"Friends? Welcome," said father, before thinking any further. Three well-dressed men entered the house and Father led them down the hallway. The door to the room in which we were sitting was closed.

The three men talked with our father and my sister's husband for over an hour. Mother made coffee for them, prepared some food and offered some brandy, as it was the tradition of that time.

"Did you hear what they were talking about?" asked my curious elder sister.

"No, no," said Mother.

When the three men left our house, my sister's husband entered our room first.

"What is going on?" my sister asked her husband.

"Wait until your father comes, and he will tell you." His eyes were focused on me.

"Why do you look at me like that?" I asked him. Then I turned to my sister and asked her:

"What makes him stare at me?" This time I was asking my sister for her husband and my brother-in-law.

"Soon we'll learn about it," said mother, who seemed to have heard something from the next room. Father's heavy steps interrupted discussion.

"Listen here! We just engaged Ema. From now on there are no more meaningless smiles. Now you are a grown up girl," he said.

Hot tears ran down my face.

"What? When? Who? But I..."

My words were cut off by my father:

"This job is done now! Soon the friends will come to exchange rings. That same day we will decide about the day of marriage."

"But no, father! I don't want to get married through matchmaking! I love a boy in my school."

My last words made Father make up his mind and he yelled:

"What? You love a boy?! You want to make me feel ashamed? You are going to marry the man we just chose!"

Hot tears were running down my face. What was happening with me? I was engaged with a person I did not know at all and he would become my future husband! Words of my school girlfriends echoed in my ears. "No, I will not get married through matchmaking! No way, never will I marry him! Never!" I said these last words between sobs.

"You will become a very beautiful bride," said mother. Smiles had abandoned her face. I looked at my elder sister's face. I saw tears in her eyes, too.

"Please, help me!" I said to my sister. "You understand how I feel?"

My words touched all my younger sisters, and I felt this when their hands were touching me. It seemed to me that by doing this they were telling me: we understand your pain, but we love you so much. "

"Father gave his word and he cannot break the promise." My sister's last words never stuck in my head, and I heard a strange roaring in my ears – *Father gave his word, Father....*

I glanced around me at each family member and all eyes were downcast. I spoke to my mother:

"Why don't you do something for me? Raise your head and look at me how much I am suffering!"

I saw tears from her eyes running down to her shaking chin.

"My dearest! Honey! This was your fate. We can't be the first to break the custom because everybody will call us names."

"I don't care at all," I said angrily, and pushed her away when she tried to hug me. My loud screaming made our father return to the room where we were gathered.

"What is going on here?"

"Ema does not agree with your decision. She wants to break the promise you made."

"Never!" said father. "The word of honor and oath can never be broken! This is the tradition for us Albanians. And I cannot break that tradition. So did my father, so am I doing and so will you inherit the Albanian tradition!"

"I hate the old traditions. I hate you, too!"

My last words seemed to have hit him straight in his heart. He became silent for a moment.

"If you want to make me feel ashamed by breaking the word of honor I gave to the new friends, you better never come back to this house!"

These were my father's last words, and silently he left the room, keeping his hand directly on his heart.

Never come back to this house! The given word can never be broken. This is the tradition of Albanians.

All those words were violently stirring my stomach. I ran straight to the bathroom and slammed the door behind me. I was throwing up and felt like somebody was pulling my heart out of my chest. My eyes were blurring and I could only stammer nonsense. Oh Lord! What is happening with me?

I heard a violent knocking on the bathroom door.

"Are you okay? Let me enter!"

I did not speak. The door opened.

"Oh God!" exclaimed my elder sister. "You have turned completely pale!"

Quickly she got some water and splashed it over my face. The cold water and my wet clothes made me come to myself, but my whole body was shaking. And mother brought some dry clothes for me.

"Pull yourself together now! It is not the end of the world!" said my mother. "Things will settle and return to normal again. You will go to school and will feel better."

My mind was blown. The school, friends, boys and girls, Arbi! How was I going to explain to them what had happened to me? How could I tell Arbi that our true love had been wounded by the old traditions of my parents? What was going to happen with us? "I can't go to school," I said coldly. "I feel like I am dying!"

"Get up," said my sister. "Dress up! Me and my husband will accompany you to school."

"You'd better return home now."

"Listen here! I love you much, therefore do not speak to me that way, please!"

As she spoke I glimpsed a tear roll down a round cheek. I looked at her with a feeling of regret. She maybe had felt like me when they had engaged her. She did not have any elder sister to embrace and help her calm down. I was too little when she was engaged and I could not understand anything then. All the girls of her age had the same fate. Now this would be my fate, too. But I, however, raised my voice and said "no" to that very backward custom. What would happen next I didn't know. I leaned on my sister and we stayed like that for a while in each other's arms.

"You will soon get used to it," said my sister. I withdrew from her arms and looked at myself in the mirror. My eyes were swollen from the tears.

"What time is it?" I asked.

"It's almost afternoon," she answered. "I am sure you are hungry now. Let's eat something before you go to school. You have to be there by four p.m."

"I know, but I don't want to go." I set at the eating table, feeling all my sisters' eyes on me while they were eating their warm soup. I only tried one spoonful, but couldn't eat anymore.

"I can't," I said and left the table.

"If you don't want to eat the soup, just try some toasted bread and cheese. Cheese would do good to your stomach," said my mother.

I went to my room, which actually was not only mine, as I shared it with two other sisters. Only our brother, being a boy, and only two years old, slept in his own room. I looked at the mirror and noticed that my face had turned pale and my eyes seemed to have sunk deeper into their sockets. A blue bruise made a line around my eyes as if somebody had hit me with a fist, though I might have felt better if it was only a fist. But it was not that simple. It was not a fist on my face. It was a fist that had hit my future like a battering ram. "Oh Lord! Great God! Please help me," I whispered to myself, looking at the ugly face of that person beyond the mirror. Then I saw the school bag thrown to the corner of the room. I took it in my hands and tried to find a photo with my classmates made during the military training. I saw myself in the first line sitting on my knees. In the second line I saw Arbi behind me.

"What will happen to both of us?" I asked the picture. "I have no idea at all how I am going to explain it to you." Talking to myself like this, I still kept crying. I heard some noise in the room. It was my elder sister.

"Get ready! We shall accompany you to school. Go and comb your hair. You look like you have just risen from the grave."

My sister seemed to have recovered herself. I put the picture into my bag, and tried to somehow make up my mind and make myself look better. It was better for me to go to school. There I could speak to my classmates. Perhaps they would help me. Perhaps Arbi himself would help me. While getting ready for school, I heard mother's voice from outside the room:

"Where? From where are those new friends?"

"From the south. They seemed to be good. The future bridegroom had seen our daughter many times, and he has fallen in love with her. Bridegroom's father had some thick eyebrows."

Father continued to tell it to my mother in a quiet voice. The word "thick eyebrows" hit me so bitterly. Was it that strange man who had followed me? Like father, like son! My God!

"Mother, was he the one who followed behind me like a ghost?"

"I don't know. But he seems serious," Mother said.

"He seems crazy and cunning," said the elder sister.

"What is done is irreversible," said Mother. "Everything is done now. You finish school and then we make the wedding."

Mother's words enraged me.

"I will never marry him! You will see! Never!"

My voice made father enter the room.

"What is happening here?" he asked.

Mother told him briefly what was happening.

"That means you already knew that boy before!" My father looked very angry.

"No," I said to him. "He has chased me."

"But you have already given him the word, is that so?"

"No, not at all. On the contrary. I have told him that I hate him and not to follow me."

"This means that the world has seen you with him! You have brought shame on us!"

"No, I said, no!"

"Listen to me," said Father. "Go to school, finish school, and never speak to any boy from now on! You are an engaged girl now. I will take you out of that school if I hear even a single word about you, okay?"

"But I don't love that man, Father! I hate him! That person has no interest in my thoughts and opinion as long as he's made everything he wants an accomplished fact."

My words surprised my father.

"That's a shame! You are opposing me, your father?" He put his hand again over his chest as if his heart was in pain.

"I gave my word and I can't break it now." These were the last words of my father. He whispered something in mother's ear and left.

"You are going to kill your father," said Mother.

"No, mother, no. He is killing me."

I grabbed my bag and left the house, not saying goodbye to anybody.

"Wait," said my sister, "I will accompany you." I did not speak and she ran after me.

"Don't worry! I swear you will feel better in a few days. Listen to me," she continued, "I was married through matchmaking, and now I have a husband and a little daughter. And I feel well, don't you think so?"

"Maybe," I said. "You may feel contented because you were not in love with anyone when you got engaged to be married."

My anger made me speak very loudly.

"Lower your voice! Who told you that I was not in love with someone else?"

"What?

"Yes, I was in love with someone else. But who would even dare tell it then? If I dared to do so, that would be considered the greatest shame. But I am proud of you. Whatever the situation is, you told the truth."

"What is the value of the truth if that doesn't change anything?"

"It makes a difference," she said. "I saw our father was thinking. He knows that this kind of tradition is wrong. But he does not want to be the first to break the tradition."

On the way to the bus station I kept thinking about these words. I had agreed with Arbi to wait for me at the station. When I arrived I saw him sitting there waiting and flipping through a magazine. He was surprised to see me accompanied. I did not approach him. I didn't know whether I was afraid of my sister or that I did not know how to explain things to Arbi. Maybe both these reasons. Arbi stood up when he saw us. Very cautiously yet decisively he approached.

"What has happened? Are you okay? Come on, tell me!" He was completely focused on me. Then he threw a quick look at my sister. I was not speaking. Just stood there like a dead tree. Tears ran down my face again. One more word from him and I was ready to burst out.

"How are you?" my elder sister said to him at last. He stretched out his hand as a sign of respect. "Good, good. My name is..."

"I know," my sister interrupted. "Ema told me everything about you."

"How nice. I am proud of you," he said to me, full of joy. "But I am not understanding why you are so worried."

I could not stand it anymore. I threw myself in his arms, weeping.

"Do not be proud for nothing!" I said and withdrew from his arms that were still holding me tightly.

"Why not? What has happened?"

My sister intervened saying, "Now I better go so that you will have it easier to speak to each other. Goodbye! Please, try to understand my sister," she told him.

"To understand what? Please, what? Speak to me!"

He did not pay any attention at all to my elder sister who was leaving the bus station.

"Sit here next to me! Whatever might have happened, you still have me. Isn't it so? Calm down now, and tell me!"

It was just those words "you have me" that brought me back to myself. I stopped weeping, held Arbi's hands and spoke, "Here is exactly what I am weeping, for my parents do not think that way. They engaged me to somebody else. You understand me? Now I am an engaged girl. Engaged! Understand? It does not matter that I love you. It does not matter that you love me. They do not care about our feelings. It is traditions they care about. If I break that tradition, I will never return home again."

I said these words very quickly and in a loud voice, and saw people turning their heads toward us. Arbi was shocked to hear this bitter surprise.

"Engaged! When? To whom?"

I had never seen Arbi angry. His eyes were burning with despair. His hands were shaking. He didn't know what to do.

"I can't believe it!" he said angrily. His gaze returned to me with tears in his eyes. Up to this moment I had never seen any man cry. This made me find some courage and I spoke:

"Please, Arbi, do not cry! I love you like crazy! Let's both go away! I hate my family now. They are the reason we are feeling like this, isn't it so, Arbi? Speak to me!" Tears in my eyes were slowly drying up, but still I was feeling the wet tear traces on my face. I raised my hand up and touched his chin.

"Please, raise your head up and tell me something!"

I continued touching his lovely face. His cheeks, shaved carefully, had become red. Here and there in the middle of that red color I could see some tiny yellow spots. I kept touching him lightly again. My fingers stopped at his swollen lips, almost dried up because of fast breathing or the blowing wind that was gaining speed. He was trembling all over. I looked around and noticed that more people were coming to the station waiting for the bus. He held my hands and said:

"Let's go somewhere!" I followed him with quick steps.

"Arbi, where are you going?" He did not speak but stopped behind a building. He grabbed for my hands. My heart was beating fast. He continued to stare me in the eyes like a madman.

"Ema!"

"Yes, Arbi...."

"I am crazy about you! I love you much! So much!"

"Me too. I love you so much!" For a moment I was happy. Without thinking anymore, I kissed him on his burning lips. He hugged me with all his strength. We both felt as if we would never separate from each other. He kissed me lightly on the forehead, and was smelling my hair. I really loved that. But I knew that his mind was whirling at the same time, or he was gaining time to think. After a while, he withdrew a bit from me and kept fixing my hair with his fingers.

"Listen to me," he said. His face had become serious:

"I love you much!"

"I know that."

"But wait," he spoke again. "Listen to me to the end, without interrupting!" He kept touching my face with his fingers.

"Okay," I said. "Go ahead!"

"If we run away somewhere together, and break the word of your parents, you will never see your family again. Isn't that so?"

"I don't care about it!" I said without thinking.

"Wait, wait! Now you are thinking this way, but I know how much you love your family, your sisters, and your little brother. It is not that simple. Besides that, you will lose your schooling. All this would mean ruin for your future. I couldn't excuse myself if I let you do this."

His words were lessening the pain in my heart bit by bit. It was true. I was so closely linked to my family up to these moments. Tears started to run again on my face as before.

"I am only seventeen years old," he continued. "Still in high school and not a single penny in my pocket. Where can I send you? How are we going to live? You are only sixteen."

He lowered his voice. "My little sweetheart! My soul!" He lifted my head up and wiped my tears with his hand. Kissed my eyes, kissed me again and again. You have your future, your life ahead. Do you hear me? I will love you for the rest of my life, but to separate you from your family or destroy your future, I cannot do that, I cannot!" He could not look at me.. "I know that this will be very difficult for me. Pure torture! But I have to do it. I have to move away from you. I must leave you in peace! You concentrate on your school and your family! Everything will be okay!"

I must have been weeping loudly because I heard Arbi whisper:

"Shush... Don't do this! It is not the end of the world!" I saw his shoulders shaking, too. He was breathing heavily and fast.

"What is happening? Oh, Great God!" I started to murmur. My first love is ending here! But why? Why must we be victims of these backward traditions?

"Pull yourself together now. We have to go! The bus is here."

"Come on! Let's go!" I said.

He grabbed my hand and asked that we walk together, but when I started to move, he released my hand at once.

"You are an engaged girl now. I'd better keep my distance from you!" he said quietly. "It is not good for you!"

Walking behind him I was looking at him with surprise and regret.

Was he really serious or not?

"So, definitely we are not lovers anymore?" I said this full of anger, pulling Arbi by his blouse and ignoring whether anybody was looking at us or not. Arbi didn't say a word. He turned quickly around, and by accident hit somebody who was hurrying to enter the bus.

"Watch out, are you blind?" he yelled at the stranger. I understood how extremely angry Arbi was now. He didn't know what to do. I jumped onto the bus, wiping tears still running down my face, and kept looking through the window. Almost everybody had gotten on the bus, except for Arbi. He remained there alone and I saw him collecting little stones from the ground and angrily throwing them away in all directions. Then he turned his head only at the last moment the bus was moving. My eyes crossed his and I noticed that he had burst into tears. Now he was understanding indeed what he had given up. Now I understood, too, how much he loved me. His red face, his tears, his trembling shoulders and his anguish showed everything.

The bus kept moving, but Arbi remained sitting there, resting both his hands on the ground. The bus was now a few hundred yards down the street and his silhouette disappeared. My tears were almost dried up on my face. I felt that I had become like a wilting tree. I arrived at the school dorm later than the time the director had told me. When I met him, he tried to judge me by asking a few questions, but when he saw that I was not answering at all, he let me go, and added:

"I don't understand what has happened to you. You better go and calm down."

I walked away in silence. Now for days on end, I kept silent at the dorm, in school, in class. Everyone was surprised by my cold attitude, but none insisted on finding out what had happened to me. Perhaps, I was thinking, it is the age, we all are 16 or 17 years old. They all are busy with their problems, or perhaps they are respecting me with their silent attitude. However, by not asking me, I felt as if they knew everything. It was only Lili and Dita who stopped me one day after school and said:

"Come on! What is wrong? Why don't you speak it out? You are not anymore the girl you used to be! Something has happened to you. What?"

"Girls, please stay away from me! Leave me in peace!" I took my bag and started to move away. Lili stood in front of me:

"You can go nowhere until you tell us! Sit here!" Her hands made me sit down on one of the benches.

"What shall I tell you?" I started, with my eyes on the ground. "To tell you that now I am engaged? Is it this you want to hear? There you are! You heard it now! Come on, and tell me what to feel!"

Both girls looked dead, frozen by what they heard. Their half-opened mouths said everything. Dita spoke first:

"What will you do now?"

"I can't do anything! Arbi doesn't speak to me anymore. He does not think that I should run away from my family, though he told me that he will love me for the rest of his life."

"So that's why Arbi does not speak to me, as he used to do before! said Dita. "Oh, how sorry I feel for you!" she continued. "You have it very difficult, no doubt, but Arbi has it even more difficult, because he is putting your interests first, without thinking about his feelings for you. Now I feel that Arbi is an even a better friend…" Dita kept talking, momentarily lost in her thoughts.

"What will you do?" said Lili, her eyes filled with tears.

"Nothing," I answered quietly, "it's over now. Arbi told me that there is no turning back anymore. There are only two things to do. Either I run away with Arbi and never see my family again, or I give up Arbi and let him pretend that nothing has happened. For my sake, he persists in saying that we cannot fight together for our happiness. He thinks that this would be a complete downfall for me."

"How do you feel now after all this has happened?" asked Lili.

"I don't know whether I feel anything right now. I feel completely numbed. I am tired of weeping. I don't know what to do. I don't know how to act. I have lost interest in learning, speaking, eating. Everything seems dead to me."

My words impressed and touched Dita, who, at that moment, was listening silently.

"You don't be foolish now! Don't do this!" With her hands on my shoulders, holding them tightly, she added, "Don't you know that you are only sixteen years old? You are so tall, beautiful, smart. Why should you worry so much? Besides that, you have us, too. Both beautiful girls, too," she joked smiling a little. Do you remember when someone from the other parallel class said to us, "Hey you, the most beautiful triple of our school!"

She continued to speak that way, trying to bring even a faint smile back on my face.

"Stop! That's enough!" I just spoke angrily without fully knowing why. "You go and tell everybody that now one of the three beautiful girls is engaged to someone whom she doesn't know at all. You tell them that my dreams are dead! Do you get it now?"

Then I grabbed my school bag and walked toward the classroom. I turned, "You'd better get up and let's go! There is nothing you can do to help me! It depends only on Arbi. Only if he agrees that we both run away somewhere far away where we can live together. Only then could I speak. For the moment I cannot speak or think of anything at all. He does not agree that this should be the solution. He thinks that we are too young. And what is most important, he cannot accept the fact that I will have to abandon my family."

I walked in silence and the girls continued to walk alongside.

"As a matter of fact, he is right. He…" said Lili.

"Give me a chance to talk once more with Arbi," Dita interrupted.

I stopped walking and turned to her:

"Please do not make such a mistake. It seems to me as if I want to push Arbi to do something he is not ready or willing to do. That's enough for now! You go home and eat something! It's almost two p.m."

"What are you going to do?" asked Lili with her beautiful eyes.

"I am going to the dormitory. I'm sure my roommates will be worried about me now.

"We love you so much, okay?"

Both girls embraced me and left, talking to each other about me for sure.

A few months elapsed. Cold winter months seemed to be even more frigid for me because of my already dead feelings. I kept dragging myself to school and returning to the dorm without any special interest. For a long time I didn't go home either. My parents visited me now and then. I did not speak much to them, but one day my mother told me:

"You have to be careful now, and don't do any foolish things, because your fiance may watch and see you. This would be a shame for us!"

"I don't care at all for him, and not even for you!"

I thought that my words would make my father angry. To my surprise, his voice was soft. He said, "Your future husband will not bother you before you finish school. That is how I have made the agreement with him. But after you finish school he has the right to come and we determine the day of the wedding."

"Perhaps he will die during this time," I said angrily.

"No, no! Don't speak like that, my daughter!"

"You'd better go now! I have nothing else to tell you."

Before leaving I let only my mother embrace me; to my father I simply said goodbye. He grumbled back goodbye to me, and I knew I had gotten to him.

A few more days passed in a cold routine. Every day I went to the classroom with my homework done so as to have less contact with teachers. My classmates did not disturb me much. In the meantime I watched Arbi every day, hoping that he might change his mind. He used to come to class very silently. He said nothing except good-morning, without addressing anyone. Then he took his seat. Now and then my eyes would cross his, but he would bend his head and pretend as if he was writing something or would turn his head to the other side. This made me furious, but there was nothing I could do. And therefore I decided to do my best to ignore him for some days. This drew his attention and he showed it openly during a French language lesson. The teacher was absent that day. Most of the classmates were talking to one another. I was pretending to do something else, though all my attention was concentrated on him. He waited for a moment hoping that I might turn my head. It was obvious that he could not resist anymore and came to the bench where I was sitting. His presence there made me tremble. My cheeks began to flush.

"Turn your head to me and look straight into my eyes!" His voice was soft, sweet and exciting.

I turned my head. He said:

"Your face has become completely red."

"Because of my anger," I said and kept scribbling on a piece of paper.

"That is not true. However," he continued, "I want you to listen to me."

"What do you have to say?"

"You know how much I want for things to flow normally for both of us, but it is impossible. I cannot resist avoiding you or not seeing you. At least allow me to take care of you. Just talk to me about any problems and I will be at your side no matter what."

"How will you be on my side?" I said, really angry. "Like a lover, or what?"

"Like a friend," he said. "Like someone who will care about you for the rest of your life."

When I heard these words I felt both anger and a deep sorrow. He was still thinking that I would have it easier that way. I grabbed his hand.

"I can't," I said. He squeezed my hand. His face had already frozen because of my unexpected action. The touch of our hands had created a powerful electricity between us. He was looking at me completely lost.

"Hey! Can you face the truth or not?"

He did, somehow, pull himself together.

"Through our common efforts we can succeed."

"Lies!" I said, without thinking. "Listen! For the time being I have it very difficult. If you don't have any other thoughts, it would be better that you stay away from me."

My words were hard. He understood very well what I was asking of him.

"No," he said point-blank. "You may think whatever you want, but I cannot destroy your dreams by taking you away from school, from your family, from everything."

"Then leave me in peace, please!" I murmured. I said that knowing with all my heart I did not want to let him walk away.

"Okay," he said, "I am leaving. But know this: I will not give up being your friend."

He stood up stiffly. I don't know whether with me or with himself. He kicked the bench on the other side with his foot, threw his bag forcibly over his bench and hurried out of the room.

I heard students calling, "What's the matter with you?" "Watch what you are doing!"

I felt very sorry when he left the room that way because I was feeling the same thing: rage and despair for a world that was destroying our dreams. I also felt anger toward Arbi. I didn't know why it seemed to me that he could do something. But my thoughts were cut off by the voice of one of my classmates, who was staring out the window.

"Hey, come and look over there!"

- I turned my head. My God! He, my beloved Arbi, quiet and always well-behaved toward everybody, was fighting with some other boys. His nose was bleeding. There were many against him in a bitter fistfight. He kept fighting back. It was obvious that he could be beaten to death. I didn't wait anymore, and ran before thinking what others would say. I hurled myself into the middle of the group, yelling out:

"Stop! That's enough! Why are you fighting? Are you out of your minds?" My intervention ended the nonsensical fight. I grabbed Arbi by his arm and said, "Are you crazy? Let's go!"

While I was speaking to him, one of those boys came close to me and said, "Now we understand—this was his lover!"

I had seen that face somewhere. He was somebody from the parallel class. He used to tease all of us in class, but nobody cared about him. He came closer to me and said, "Shall we go out together this week?"

I did not answer and kept pulling Arbi by his crumpled shirt. As Arbi took a first step forward, the boy from the other class moved closer and closer. He said, "Perhaps you will let me bite those full lips of yours..." He laughed with a cunning look. I spat in his face and yelled, "Away with you!"

"Uh! The beauty is angry! That's how I like it!" said that son of a bitch. I was trying to hurry away. His arm stretched out to grab my hair, and he pulled me toward his body, saying:

"Even your saliva is sweet. Who knows how sweet you are down there?" His other hand was reaching for my body. I turned toward Arbi. This last action of that villain could turn Arbi into a true beast.

"Release her! Now!" said Arbi cold as ice.

"I don't release her before I try her .... lips...." His words were cut off by Arbi's powerful fist striking him on the face. He fell to the ground with his nose bleeding and seemingly broken.

"Who else wants to get some?" He glanced around at the other boys, who, scared indeed, moved away from Arbi. "Come on over here! With this rage I have right now I will bury you alive!" His eyes were shooting sparks. Tight-fisted, he was trembling all over.

"Let's go!" I told him, somehow feeling ashamed about this whole thing. He obeyed.

"Yes, we go," he said with a grim smile. I felt very proud of him. I wanted to throw myself into his arms, to embrace him, to kiss him. He was walking quietly beside me, giving me the same affectionate look.

"Why did you stop that fight?" he asked me, "You could have been hurt."

"I could not stand it when I saw you in that situation. What made you fight with those stupid scoundrels?"

"I don't know why. I was so desperate. And they provoked me at a very bad moment. I couldn't stand it anymore And that self-conceited jerk was the last straw. I almost went crazy. Same thing will happen to all those who dare touch you again."

His words made me feel warm somehow. I knew that he was the same Arbi he had been before. In love with me.

I tried to provoke more feeling from him. Staring straight into his eyes I said, "And you do all this simply because we are friends?"

He slowed his steps. The corridor was quiet. He turned to me and his look penetrated through me. I felt my heart beating heavily.

"You already know," he said. "Don't you feel it? It is more than friendship. It is more than love. It is something even more…which I cannot name."

"It is both of the two." I spoke with a rasp which seemed to come from a wounded heart. Silence ruled the moment. Two drops ran down my face. I was looking at Arbi, who was breathing heavily and trembling. He was standing in front of me. For a moment he closed his eyes, then he took a deep breath and said:

"Oh! How much I want to kiss you!"

"Then what are you waiting for?"

"I cannot, I can't!" His hand reached out to wipe my tears. Each touch of his hand eased a little piece of my soul. I was feeling so good. Quietness, warmth, love, protection, were all mixed together.

"I love you much, so much!" I looked away.

"I know, I know it." He spoke in a quiet voice and held my hand. "Let's go to the classroom," he said. Before entering the room, he stopped.

"Listen here!" he said. "I will love you for the rest of my life! You hear me? Wherever you may be!"

I looked straight into his big eyes in tears again. I did not speak. I wanted to say something, but couldn't. Actually he had already made his decision. I did not want to push him further. My anger had turned into respect. The door of the class was opened from the inside and we both found ourselves unprepared in front of the whole class that, to our surprise, surrounded us with applause.

"Here you are! This is what love really means," said one of the classmates, who was the most comical student of the class.

The whole class knew about our feelings, but none provoked us.

"Kisses - kisses – kisses," a voice came from the middle of the crowd. All the rest began to chant: "kisses - kisses...."

I didn't feel ashamed at all. I approached Arbi and just waited for him to do what the class asked. He grabbed both my hands, kissed them and said, "Please, do sit, all of you! Me and Ema are good friends. I will respect her all my life." After having said this, he embraced me tightly as if saying goodbye to me. Then he sat down on his bench and began trying to take something out of his school bag.

Echoes of disappointment came from the class, as they were actually expecting something else. I also had expected that Arbi would change his mind. But now I spoke out, "Listen here! Arbi is right. Now I am engaged. Arbi, and all of you here, must help me in these difficult moments. I don't know what to do. However, I have you, at least. I have you, Lili, and you, Dita. And I have Arbi." My voice became softer. Without understanding it, I had already joined Arbi's side. "Friends only," I said, stretching my hand out to him. He stood up as if bitten by a snake. But he stretched out his hand, and held mine fast.

I understood that, though he had already made his decision, he did not expect that I would accept it. He was not happy at all with this. Surprised and angry, he seized a piece of paper, crumpled it and threw it angrily toward the chalkboard.

I don't really know why I settled for a friendship with Arbi. Perhaps I had gotten tired of being alone on this adventure with him. Or, maybe, I did it to provoke Arbi's nerves and make him change his mind. And I don't know, either, what pushed me to accept the fact that now I was engaged.

A few days dragged on as I kept questioning how and why I accepted the engagement. I would ask this question to myself while looking at the mirror, or anytime I was alone. The same question, the same answer: I was an idiot.

As the weeks passed we started somehow to get used to respecting each other in class. No one was asking us about our relationship anymore. Arbi started to come to class rather quietly and not discussing anything at all. He had changed much and seemed to be somehow colder with me. I was not seeing that very special smile he used to give me. But still I was hoping to hear the clicking of his pen as he used to do before. That was one of our signals to look each other in the eyes. Or sometimes he would clear his voice to tell me that he was there. None of these were happening anymore. I did not like it, but had no choice. Last of all, I had already accepted that "we are only friends now." However, within me the love for Arbi never died, irrespective of that foolish decision I had made to be "friends." I would eagerly wait to see him anytime. Each day I even cared whether he had prepared the lessons or done his homework before coming to class. If not, we did them before the lesson began. This gave me the chance to be near him for a few minutes. Somehow we got used to that daily routine.

We were approaching the end of the second school year, and we had already grown pretty much. Boys had become taller and had developed the man-like look. Girls had become more beautiful. Now they were taking better care of themselves. It was week of exams and all of us were studying most of the time. After lessons we ate lunch and went to study again. Same would happen in a usual day. One afternoon I had gone up to my room and was discussing with my girlfriends about next day's lessons.

"You help me in composition and I will help you in algebra," said Eli. "You don't do anything at all in math," she joked.

"You have only numbers rolling around in your head," I answered laughing. "When it comes to theory, literacy or history, you are nil." At that moment I heard someone calling:

"Ema, somebody wants you downstairs."

They wanted me downstairs?! Who can that be? I met my parents yesterday. I ran down the steps to see who was asking for me. I looked around. Was it someone I knew? I saw no one. I went to the person on duty at the entrance.

"Who asked for me?"

The boy on duty spoke:

"He's over there." He pointed with his finger.

I turned my head in that direction. I had seen that face before, and was trying to remember where I had seen him.

"Who are you?" I asked him, without moving an inch from my place.

He stepped forward, "It is me."

His devilish smile and his thick eyebrows reminded me that it was he, the 'fiance.'

"What do you want here? You know that you are not allowed to come here before I finish school. That's how the agreement is between my father and you. Or don't you know that?" I didn't even know this clown's name.

"It is true," he said, "but I thought I might come and meet you and we could get to know each other. Or, am I wrong?"

"If it was for me," I interrupted quickly, "I don't want to know you at all. I don't understand how you may have a feeling for a person you don't know at all either. And it is much worse in my case. You'd better give up that damned engagement! Besides that, how can you marry a girl who is in love with someone else for two years now?" I wasn't ashamed or scared at all to tell him that. I hated him and had reason, because he was the initiator and the cause of that undesirable engagement.

"That is not true," he reacted, choking with anger. "You!? You making love with someone? That is a lie!"

"Every day after lessons we make love," I continued, "and therefore get away from me!"

However, it was obvious that my words were not true, though I tried to sound convincing for him. He did not trust me.

"Palavers," he said quietly. "I know why you tell me all this. Just to get rid of me. Stop with these things because you can't deceive me. Let's take a walk together."

"Me, walking with you? Never! It's true you are my fiance, but I will never love you! It is better that you leave me at peace!"

"No, I will not do that. I will wait until you finish school. After that you will be mine." He was definitely very angry.

"Yatata … yatata …" I shouted, "I will never become yours! You'd better change your mind! Go and find someone else!"

I hurried away from him and did not hear his supplications.

"Who was he?" I heard my friends asking me.

"It was just a body with two ears," I said. My girlfriends laughed, but did not push me any further in the matter.

The second year of high school was over. During the summer holidays I helped my parents at home.

"This year you will not go out anymore with boys like before," said my mother.

"And why not?"

"Because the world would laugh at us. Now you are given to a husband." While talking, my mother moved and banged things in her kitchen.

"What husband, mother? I am still a child!"

"Boo, boo! You will discredit us; you will bury us alive if you cause such a shame! Not to speak of your father, who has already got heartache! You have to make up your mind, my daughter!" I had rarely heard Mother so worried.

"I have absolutely made up my mind," I said. "You are almost out of your mind! You can't get it!"

Gradually, in time, I started to feel hatred for my parents. Why didn't they fight for their daughter? I was not able to understand.

One day our uncle came to visit us. He was drinking his coffee while talking to our father. I loved uncle very much. He was reasonable and wise. All listened to him whenever he spoke. His smoking pipe was continuously releasing wispy smoke. He never took it out of his mouth, and often smoke seemed to rise with his every breath. You would think he should have asthma.

"Bring me a glass of water, Ema!" he said to me with a cough. Feeling glad that I could speak to him, I hurried to bring him the glass of water.

"What is wrong with you? Are you okay?" I said, placing my hand on his shoulder.

"I am well, dear child. Don't worry! Death cannot find me. What about you? How are you?"

- My uncle's question caught me unprepared. What if I told him about my engagement? Maybe he would help me.

"How can I be well, uncle? They have engaged me with someone I don't love. And they don't change their mind about this decision."

"Listen here!" he said. "You are young. Today it seems unjust to you. Besides that, dear child, we cannot be the first to break the rules of the Canon. The village would call us names…"

"Why not?" I asserted quickly. "Someone has to break it. Why not? Why can't we be the first?"

I don't know why my words caused a silence for a few moments.

Finally my uncle said, "You are going to make a very beautiful bride! You will get used to it, daughter. Your grandmother did. So did your own mother. And now it is your turn to respect the Canon and its laws. Come on, okay?"

I began again to object.

"You go to your room now," said Father, who seemed to be looking for support from our uncle. In fact, the uncle kept silent for a long time. While walking away from him I saw his smoke rings rising slowly to the ceiling.

Why couldn't my uncle help me—convince my father to cancel that cursed engagement?

From the next room I heard my uncle say, "Ah, our dear daughter!"

What did "Ah, our dear daughter" mean?

The room door was closed from the inside; the heavy old door seemed to be heavier because of the weight of secrets being told in that very room.

Later, on his way out of the house, I heard uncle say, "We will prepare a wonderful big wedding."

- He, too, had proved to be a slave to tradition.

My summer holidays went by without any special event. When back to school, I didn't have anything to tell my friends. When they asked how I had enjoyed the holidays, I told them that almost everything had been meaningless. In the meantime I heard Lili saying that she had met someone and that she had fallen in love at first sight. Dita, too, was speaking passionately about a boy from the upper classes of the school. "Happy you!" I whispered.

"Aren't you glad for us?" The two girls spoke in unison.

"Very glad," I said, "but I don't know whether it will be possible to have your dreams come true. Just look at me." I knew I was oozing with self-pity.. "You may think that I don't love Arbi. I love him much, very much. But all this is useless when I have no control of my life. Possible luck and happiness of girls in this country are in the hands of somebody else. Therefore they say that even the tree leaves weep when a girl is born." I used this expression because I'd heard it from my mother recently.

"I do not care at all," said Lili, her head in the clouds. "I don't know what will happen tomorrow. I am in love with him and I am the happiest person in the world."

Then I heard Dita say "Yeees!" and she raised her hands up in the air to join Lili's hands in an expression of agreement.

"Nevertheless, careful girls, be careful! You know now what happened to me."

"But this doesn't mean that it's going to happen to us, too," said Dita.

"Well then, okay. I will not talk anymore about it. I'm very happy for you. Now tell me what happened, when and where? First tell me, who are these good boys who have won your hearts?"

We burst into laughter. It had been a long time since I laughed like that. While they were telling their stories, I was thinking about Arbi. Where might he be now? Days had passed since school started and Arbi had not been seen yet. What had happened to him?

"Do you know anything about Arbi?" I asked them in a low voice.

"Oh," said Dita, "yesterday I spoke with him. He does not want to come to this class anymore. He wants to go to the other parallel class. And if that is not arranged, he will not come to school at all."

"What?" I stood up. "I can't believe it! He must not quit school now! It is the third school year."

"I told him the same," said Dita. "It seems that he finds it difficult to be in the same class with you." Quickly I wrote a short note to him:

"Please meet me tomorrow at the park. I want to talk to you. It is very important. Will be waiting for you at 2 pm." I folded the paper and put it into Dita's jacket pocket.

"Please, give this note to Arbi!"

"Surely," said Dita.

Next day I felt like I was sitting on thorns until the last lesson of the day was over. Immediately, I ran straight to the park where I should meet Arbi, hoping that he'd be there waiting for me. Being a bit tired, I sat on a stool and kept turning my head looking for him. I did not see anybody yet. A sad feeling prevailed. I would wait a little longer. Maybe this kind of waiting was not for girls. Girls are more fragile and more sensitive. Nonsense! How would I know how boys feel?

I stood up and turned my head to the path to see if Arbi was coming. I only saw my own lonely shadow. What was I waiting for? He is angry with me! Maybe he got another girl! What did he want from me? Must I wait for him his whole life?

My shadow did not speak, did not give me any answers. I slapped myself hard across the face. Must you go crazy? Pull yourself together! I grabbed my bag and started to walk toward the school dorm.

I had only walked about 100 meters when I heard a familiar voice. "Wait! Please, do not leave!"

It was Arbi. My face, my eyes and lips, were suddenly beyond my control. I was smiling. I could not hide my joy.

I tried to speak in a serious manner, "Where were you?"

"I was here. I was around." He said it in a low voice. "Let's go and find a place where we can talk in privacy."

I obeyed his words, though I did not see any people around us. We sat somewhere on the grass. Everything around was green. Here and there you could see some flowers in the park that seemed to desire to prolong their lives even now in September. The grass we were sitting on was soft like cotton. It was very relaxing.

"What's up?" he said.

"Nothing," I told him, feeling like I was lost somewhere. I'd forgotten that it was I who had asked for this meeting. I don't know why I was keeping my head down. Maybe I wanted to hide that blush I would get each time I was near him. I felt Arbi's breath close to my face.

"Speak. You had something to tell me." His voice was soft.

"Oh, yes. Why don't you come to school? What happened to you? Is everything okay with your family?"

I was looking straight at his face. His appearance seemed abnormal. His curly hair seemed uncombed and his eyes looked tired. I was used to seeing him always carefully shaved, but this time maybe he had not shaved for a few days. He was looking at me speechlessly.

"Arbi, you must come to school. Do you hear me?" I was trembling.

"I hear you very well."

"Then why don't you speak?"

He looked down for some seconds, then brought his eyes up and put his palms on his face.

"What shall I say? I can't. What shall I tell you? That I am crazily in love with you and that I am not able to do anything at all? I have not a penny to start life with you. I have no house. I have nothing, nothing! In some way I compelled you to accept that cursed engagement." His face was full of anger.

I saw his lips were quivering.

"Therefore I have not come to school. I have no solution whatsoever for us. Do you understand it now?"

"I know that you have it difficult, but you must come to school. You made a decision to protect my interests so that I can finish school.

And you have to do the same for yourself. First finish school, and then we'll wait and see. I was speaking calmly and in a decisive tone. You are smart and your future lies ahead. Tomorrow I want to see you in school! Do you hear me?"

I shook him by his shoulders as if to make him pull himself together. "Life continues, Arbi. At least, if you do so, I will see you every day. If I need your help, you are there in class. Isn't it so?"

"Yes, yes. That is true." The faintest smile appeared on his wet face.

"You are the strongest person that I know," he said.

"And you are the most beloved person in the world," I said, laughing. "Now go home and get prepared for tomorrow. I will be waiting for you in class. Promise me that you will come!"

"Okay, okay," he said, and stood up, helping me to do the same. We embraced each other like two good friends. While leaving that place, I turned my head and said:

"Don't you forget!"

"Okay, see you tomorrow."

Glad for my success, I hurried my steps toward the dormitory.

The next morning I eagerly waited for classes to begin.

Was he coming? I did not enter the classroom for a long time. Many students coming to school simply greeted me good morning. I answered without paying any attention to them.

And there he was, surrounded by a group of friends. He saw me from far away and greeted me with a little wave. That's what I wanted. I entered the classroom thinking that everything would be okay. And that was so, indeed. The whole third school year went well and full of activities. There was not much time for us to cause any foolishness. At least I call it so now.

One of the most beautiful activities that I will remember for the rest of my life was when all three parallel classes visited one of the southeast cities of the country. I had always wanted to visit that city. The youth at that time called it the city of serenades. We traveled there by train.

On the train Arbi was sitting in front of me. On my side I had one of the dorm's caretakers - a man in his 40s. On Arbi's side sat two female classmates. All the way to the city we were singing or playing different games. I was very happy. Now and then my feet would touch Arbi's. I withdrew them quickly as if to show that it happened unconsciously. We were playing cards very passionately. When someone would try to cheat, we yelled loudly to one another. Once I thought that the other party had done some unjust play, and I just threw my cards over the small train table.

"I don't want to play anymore!"

"Come on! This is just a game," said Arbi, grabbing my hands. His touch gave me a pleasant feeling.

"Okay. But I'll be watching you closely, mister." I slid my hands from his, though honestly I wanted to hold them the whole trip. He seemed to have understood my desire and stretched his legs with a quick move and put one of my legs between his. And I did not withdraw it. He continued the game with others and now and then squeezed my leg as if to say: I am here with you. I threw my eyes on him for a moment and saw that he seemed completely aware only of me. I don't know how I appeared, but I also felt a special feeling. It was a kind of pleasure that overpowered me all over. I was sitting close to the person I loved and did not feel ashamed at all to touch him or let him touch me.

"Do you want to eat something?" asked the dorm caretaker, who had already begun to understand something. "They sell excellent sand-wiches here."

"Okay. Then let's order them for all of us around this table," he said.

We all ate and enjoyed the sandwiches.

- On our side of the bus we couldn't help hearing jokes by two boys who wanted to make us laugh. They were students at the college, but our caretaker did not appreciate their presence with us.

"Careful boys, careful!" he would say now and then.

Somebody threw a folded piece of paper to our table. The caretaker, sitting next to us, opened and read it loudly :

"I am falling in love with the girl at the end of the table. Please tell me her name before I die for her! From Toni."

The caretaker responded, "Now you are overacting, boys!"

"I took the letter, unfolded it, and, in front of everybody's eyes I wrote, "Thank you, but the only boy I love is sitting in front of me."

I folded the letter again and threw it back to the table on the other side. The boy opened it quickly and said, "Congratulations, my friend, congratulations!"

"What?" asked Arbi, who seemed not to have been able to read the letter.

"That girl in front of you loves you, not me," said the student on my side.

"This one here?" said Arbi, looking straight into my eyes. "I don't believe it."

I was also looking at Arbi straight in the eyes. He was smiling.

"All the time she was right in front of me and I did not understand it? How foolish of me!" he continued.

All were laughing loudly. And the student on the other side understood that what Arbi was doing was simply a game. "That's enough with these jokes now," said the caretaker, who seemed to be hiding a certain enjoyment for these flirtations. He was not harsh at all. Now and then, he just tried to tame our extreme enthusiasm a little.

"You are not like the others," I said.

"I know," he said, "I was once young like you. Besides that, I know your father, too."

When he said I know your father, I became quite scared.

"Please, do not tell my father that I love a boy, because he would take me out of school."

"No, I don't tell him anything. But rest assured that he knows everything."

"Do you have daughters?" I asked him.

"Yes," he said. "I have one. She is only one year old now."

"Never engage her by arranged marriage. Let your daughter choose her happiness herself. In that way she will love you more."

"That's okay. Calm down now," he added, seeing that our discussion was taking a serious tone.

In the meantime the girls of our group were heard singing:

We'll go, we'll go
To the heart of the forest
Where birds build
Their love's nest !

I did not wait but just started, in a low voice, to sing that touching song. The whole group was singing. It really was a magic moment. Though the trip lasted over three hours, to me it seemed very brief. All the time in the city we stayed together. We had some other people in the group, but the two of us were never separated. We walked silently for a while. Streets of the city were paved with cobblestones. It was a clean and very green city. As a group we visited an old factory. After that we separated to different narrow neighborhood roads of the city. Me and Arbi chose our own alley, and I don't know how long we walked together, lost in a special pleasure that was filling our hearts. We stopped in a park and sat on a bench.

"Where might the others be?" said Arbi just to break the silence.

"I don't know, but don't worry. We all will meet at the city clock-tower at six p.m."

"Why should I worry?" asked Arbi. "As a matter of fact I would like to get lost so that nobody could find us."

"I was thinking the same thing," I said.

"Do you know that this city is near the border with another state? If we trespass the border we would be the happiest people in the world."

"Yes, but have you forgotten the ways of the "gentle" communists? If we fail to pass to the other side they would put us in prison like two traitors. I can't imagine the reason for the law but whoever breaks it is sentenced to death."

While I spoke, Arbi was picking up smooth stones and throwing them at birds. He seemed to be nervous. I always knew; he was no good at hiding it.

"But now I am here with you."

The view around us was deliberately provoking. The sun rays and a light breeze were fondling our hair. Birds were playing and singing with their fascinating voices. Flowers were so beautiful in that park that even the most talented painter would not have found those rare colors spread so naturally all over the park. Plunged in the fascinating beauty of nature, our faces were now close to each other. He bent his head a little ways down just to come even closer. His lips touched mine. Oh! How long had I waited for that moment once again! That kiss was sweet, warm. I felt a sweetness in my lips as if I had just bitten a cherry full of juice. Surely, he was feeling the same. One more kiss, one more. Oh, how much I wanted that moment to never end!

"I feel like the happiest person in the world," he said. "And you?"

I smiled and said:

"I don't know."

"What don't you know?" he asked and fondled my red nose with his fingers. Then he whispered in my ear, "You seem to be confused and completely lost."

The way he whispered made me jump up. I could not hide my feelings and lie to Arbi. I had always told the truth.

"But you know how I feel for you."

"How do you feel? He asked.

"I feel happy, and it seems to me that I have no other problems at all when I am with you. I feel protected from anything bad taking place in this world." I kissed him lightly on the lips.

"Is that all?" he said after kissing me back.

I didn't say a single word. Instead other hot kisses followed, sometimes light and exciting, sometimes powerful and passionate. While our lips kept meeting again and again, I murmured half-words: This enough? What about this? And this?

For a moment he seemed shocked and confused by my courage and continued to kiss me like crazy. When I stopped talking, he took me in his arms and said, "Let's go somewhere."

"Release me, please! Let me walk myself!" I said, laughing loudly. He let me free, still holding my hand tight. His eyes were twinkling with a special spark. He repeatedly pulled me tight to his body.

"Where shall we go?" I asked him.

"To a quieter place," he said. "Look over there, at the end of the park there is a little hill. I don't think there will be anybody moving around. We can talk there. We both began running hand in hand not knowing for sure what would happen next. After some minutes we stopped under the shade of an old olive tree. I turned my head around, enjoying the beauty. The whole hill was covered by olive trees. All the trees were placed the same distance from one another. From the foot of that hill the park stretched out and looked like a carpet embroidered by the best tailors in the city. It really was a fascinating view.

"What a true beauty it is!" I said. He stood there looking all around the park.

"You are very right," he said after a moment. Then he picked up some thin twigs from the olive tree full of small white flowers, and he made a little wreath and put it on my head.

"My princess," he said. "Today has been the most beautiful day of my life." While speaking, his hand was fixing my dense hair under the wreath. I felt like a princess, indeed. His hand kept caressing me slightly. Each touch of his hand felt like a light, sweet flutter. I was wondering what was happening to me? He understood that I was almost lost. He sat down and turning his face to the top of that old olive tree, said,

"Look over there!" He was lying down now carelessly and was looking amazed at the top of the tree.

"Come here near me!"

I lay down next to him holding his hand tight in mine. My body kept a certain distance from him, but my head was quite close to his.

"What are you looking at?" I asked.

"Up there," he said, pointing with his finger.

"I looked up and saw two beautiful birds playing, chirping, and jumping through the branches of the tree."

"It's me and you," I said, trying to catch his thoughts.

"Yes, my soul," he said, turning on his side. His leg went over mine. Half my body was covered by his body. I felt something strong that moved within me. A strange feeling passed through my body, something I had never sensed in my life. While kissing me, his hand, slightly caressing my neck first, went down to stop on my chest, which was moving up and down and ready to burst at any moment.

"You are very beautiful," he whispered, kissing me again. Quickly I turned around and our two bodies were joined together. I put my head on his chest and he held me tight, very tight.

"Don't be afraid," he said, trying to see me in the eyes. "I am not doing anything to you, though I am dying of that desire!" He was smiling with not an atom of shame.

Not separating my body from his, I raised my head and said: "Arbi!"

"Yes, my soulmate," he said. "I hear you."

"I have never done... you know, that, therefore I am very scared. I don't know what is going to happen."

"I know," he said, "but why are you crying?"

Somehow though I fought it, two teardrops ran down my hot cheeks and stopped at the edge of my lips.

"It's because I like everything I do with you, but something prevents me from taking a final step."

"Do not worry, my little baby. I do not do anything to you if you don't want to. I know what prevents you. It is our tradition that girls should be virgins before marriage. Next thing that prevents you is the fear of what will happen later. But of one thing you must be sure. I do nothing against your desire. Besides that, I will never urge you forcefully to do anything, irrespective of the desire and passion I have for you."

His words gave me somehow the feeling of assurance about everything.

"And therefore I love you so much, very much," I said and embraced him.

"Now we had better go," he said, standing up. "I am sure others are looking for us." His last words made me jump to my feet.

"How do I look?" I asked Arbi, fixing my hair and brushing a few leaves from my clothes.

"Very deeply in love," he said, laughing loudly. I laughed, too, and, after cleaning my clothes, said, "Wait a second. You have something here on your face."

"What?" he asked.

I kissed him and started running before him down the steps out of the park.

"Aha!" he called, running after me and catching up. He embraced me and said, "No matter how events take their course, and wherever you will be, I will love you for the rest of my life."

After a long hug we continued walking silently. Somewhere along the way we met a group of our class together with the caretaker of the dormitory. As soon as they saw us, they ran to us.

"Where have you been? It's more than an hour that we have been looking for you." We glanced at each other, somehow frightened.

"We were here in the park."

"All have got together and are waiting for you," said the caretaker, quite angry. "Your class teacher has become wild. Who knows what she thinks?"

"But we didn't do anything bad, nothing wrong." This time I spoke like an idiot.

"Oh Great God!" burst out the caretaker, made the cross, and hurried to the others who were waiting for us. When we arrived there, all students had gotten together in groups. Teachers had gathered in a separate group a few steps away from students. We joined the students, who, to our surprise, did not judge us for what had happened.

"What has happened?" I asked Dita, who held a finger in her mouth, very nervous.

"Oh God!" she exclaimed. "I don't know, but all the teachers seem very concerned. Especially our class teacher. She asked us many times about you."

"About me? Perhaps because I was late?"

"Perhaps," she said.

Very worried, I was looking for Arbi. All the others were together, except for Arbi, who was staying away from them. The principal was next to him. I don't know what he was telling him, but Arbi was moving his hands as if explaining things to him. But what? I wondered. While I stared at them, someone came from behind and touched my shoulder.

"Come with me!" It was the wild voice of the dorm guardian. Frightened, I followed her with hesitating steps. We entered a small room in the dwelling where it was planned for us to sleep the next three nights.

"You sit here!" she continued.

"I am okay standing here," I said.

"Don't you feel ashamed?" she started to yell at me. "How dare you disappear hours on end alone with that other idiot? Where have you been? What did you do? Tell me everything, otherwise you will be expelled from school!"

"But you told us that we were free until six p.m."

I was actually speaking with half a voice, but I continued, "As a matter of fact we all went away in different directions to visit the museum city." But before I finished the speech, she hit me so hard on my face that I felt as if my eyes were throwing out sparks.

"Shut your mouth, you shameless slut!" she shouted and did not let me speak. "Tell me now what you did, otherwise I am going to strangle you with my own hands!"

Her screaming terrified me.

"I don't know what to tell you. We had a walk through the city and stopped at a park and just talked."

"Go ahead! Tell me more!" It was as if she was expecting something terrible to come out of my mouth.

"I have nothing else to tell," I added. Now I was crying because of that hard slap she gave me on the face.

"Nothing? Did you make any plans to escape the country? Speak out! Tell me! I will rip your hair off, if you don't!"

Suddenly she grabbed my hair and shook my head left and right.

"I will throttle you with my hands."

I was almost going crazy with anger because of this violence she was using on me.

"Stop hitting me! We have not made any plans. I have done nothing wrong." Another fist struck my other cheek.

"Tell me now!"

She was screaming like a beast. I was shaking all over. Partly of fear and partly from the blows of her fists.

"I am party secretary," she said. "I never let plots develop under my nose."

"Plots?" I asked. "Excuse me, but it seems I am not understanding you. Besides that, I am a daughter of a member of that party."

She did not expect that answer and was shocked for a moment.

"To whom are you talking like that?"

She kept yelling and staring at me with her goggled eyes.

"Tell me everything, everything that happened with you and that other idiot. Tell what you talked about! Tell...." She now kept hitting me on my head and arms with a wooden ruler. Maybe because of pain or perhaps of the outrage, I screamed as much as I could.

"I have nothing to tell you. I have done nothing! And don't torture me like we're back in the Third Reich. Even my mother has never hit me! Who gives you the right to torture me? If I did something bad, there are rules and laws that the dormitory board handles, not you." I told her all these words in one breath. Her eyes goggled even worse this time.

"I can't believe such a thing! I can't believe it!" she screamed wildly. "Right now I am going to request that you be expelled from school and dormitory. Away with you now! I never want to see your face again!"

Suddenly, I was feeling rather calm, and I had the answers to her on the tip of my tongue,

"You may expel me from the dormitory because you are in charge of it, but you cannot expel me from school." I was speaking very decisively and quietly.

"We'll see," she said, leaving the room like a wild beast. "Right now I will inform your parents."

Her last words hit me hard. Oh, no! My parents would be alarmed for no reason. I was shaken completely. It was the fear that my parents would learn about this, the fear I might be expelled from school, and who knows what else? My God! What was going to happen to me?

My tutelary teacher came in. Her name was Pranvera. She was in her 60s. I had noticed her to always be a calm person. She had never called me down for anything. As soon as I saw her, I threw myself in her arms as if she was my mother. And she, as if understanding everything about me, said, "Don't shake like that! It is not a big deal! I trust in everything you say. Go and join the others!"

Her warm words encouraged me, though I was still crying in deep pain. She handed me a handkerchief from her pocket, and after that took off the woolen tricot she had on, and gave it to me.

"You can return it tomorrow. You go now! Come on, my soul!" she said in a soft voice. It seemed to me like the sweet voice of my mother. I embraced her again.

"Go now, go! Everything will be fixed."

I walked away to meet my class group. While walking, I turned my head back and said,

"Thank you for the trust you have in me, and for the tricot!" She waved her hand.

"Go, join the others! We'll speak later."

When I came out it was almost dark. As soon as my class group saw me, they all surrounded and bombarded me with questions.

"What has happened? What did they tell you? Why is your nose bleeding?"

I looked each one of them in the eyes. I saw Lili with her beautiful eyes filled with tears. I saw Dita, too, looking with her alarmed eyes at the dormitory guardian as if she wanted to eat her alive. All were looking at me with compassion. I didn't understand what happened either, and was trying to explain it to myself.

"She thinks that we had made a plan to escape the country, or something else." Saying this I turned my head toward the dormitory guardian. "She also thinks that I have had sex with Arbi but..."

- "Why didn't you do that?" interrupted the same humorist of our class. All laughed.

"You still remain a little child," I said to him. "These are very serious things."

"I know," he said, "but I wanted to make you laugh. I am sorry," he added, and hugged me gently. "I love you both, you and Arbi. If they expel you or Arbi from school, we all will leave this school, too. Come on! Do I look serious to you now?" He said this very proudly.

"Yes, very much so. But this problem is mine only, and I don't want the whole class to lose a diploma for my sake. Here in school, or outside this school, I will love you all my life. I will not forget any one of you. I thank you all! And you will be the first to receive the school diploma. I am sure about that. I included Zaimir in my little speech, whom I used to call the humorist of the class.

However, this time he proved that he was both a humorist and courageous, too. I hugged him and told him, "Go and see what is happening with Arbi, please."

He left by making the sign, "Yes, Madam."

I did not get any answer about what happened to Arbi either that night, or the last night in the city. The last day of the trip I stayed in my bed to rest. I was almost exhausted from everything that had happened to me. And the last night became another anxiety for me. Actually it was planned to organize an evening party with all the parallel classes of the same age from the schools of the city. I saw the girls preoccupied and standing in front of mirrors. I didn't feel at all interested in going to that party.

"Get up and dress yourself. Enough with thinking now!" said Eli, my room-mate.

"I can't," I said quietly.

"Get out of that bed and dress yourself, I say!" She grabbed me by the arm and pulled me away.

"Watch out! You are going to throw me out of bed," I told her.

"It would be even better for you to pull yourself together and come. And you never know," she continued. "Perhaps we might see Arbi there, or we may hear something more about him."

Eli's idea seemed very interesting to me. I jumped out of bed and dressed myself without any special care. I put on some narrow black slacks, and a long blouse, which covered my capricious buttocks, as my mother used to call them. Still I saw that something was missing. I looked more sportive, not proper enough for the Party. I noticed that Eli was surprised, and said, "What are you doing? Come on! Put on a nice dress!"

- "I don't, I dooon't feel good with a dress."

"But it's a dancing party."

"Who cares?" I said, turning toward the other girls.

"Okay, okay! But wait a second! Put this black belt around your bosom. Yes, that's nice now." The girl who was putting the belt on me, was Jolanda, a blonde who always dressed nicely and was known among the girls for the taste she had in combining dresses.

"Now you look more beautiful than ever," she said, pushing my hair up.

"Slow down!" I said, "Next thing you'll tell me is that I'm a top model." Then I turned to the mirror. As a matter of fact I liked myself, though my eyes looked tired.

When all were ready to go out, we heard the voice of that witch - the dorm guardian,

"Girls, all of you go down to the party hall now! Did you hear me? I don't want anyone absent. Hurry up!" Her strict tone almost killed my desire to go with the girls.

Oh, no! Her again? What shall I do? I sat on an empty chair. I didn't want to see her face!

"She has to feel bad and apologize, not you," said Eli decisively, as if she knew everything. "You did nothing, but she treated you like a criminal. Just to make her crazy, you stand up and keep your head high proudly! Let's go, girls," she said in a commanding tone. "You get up now!" she said to me, and pulled me by the hand.

And we did so. We entered the big hall, where the music sounded very normal, though I had thought that the party would be very noisy. All the students were sitting around in groups. The teachers had spread here and there among them.

"Do you see anything?" I asked the girl next to me.

"There he is," said Dita, pointing with her finger to Arbi. He stared at me for a second and then looked down. Who knew how much they had tortured him.

"At least I know that he is here now," I told Dita.

"Enjoy yourself now! Don't think anymore!" She was the first one who stood up and went dancing with a boy who asked her.

Most of the girls were dancing but quite a few were still sitting. I remained sitting there all alone, and felt sad for a moment. Why didn't Arbi get up and ask me if I wanted to dance with him? I was pretending to drink something. At that very moment someone came to me and asked, "May we dance together?"

I looked up and answered without thinking much, "Sorry, I can't."

He left somehow offended. Less than two minutes later someone else came and sat next to me.

"What's up?" he said. He was a polite boy elegantly dressed like an official. To my surprise, he looked to be in his 20s.

"What do you want here?" I said. "You are not even our age." I spoke without looking straight at him. Instead I continued watching my friends dancing.

"You are right. I come from the Central Committee. I am the secretary for the Youth organization of this city. Can we talk while dancing, please? You attracted my attention. You look very beautiful, but sad."

When he mentioned Central Committee, an idea came to my mind. I might explain to him my story. He could understand how bureaucratic and backward was the guardian of our dormitory.

"Still thinking? Shall we dance, or not?" He stood up and held my hand. "Please," he said again.

I stood up. He gave me a sweet smile and put his hand around my waist. His other hand held mine gently. He danced beautifully.

"Raise your head up," he said, after some routine dancing rotations. "I like girls who are very light dancers."

"Keep your distance, please," I said, this time looking into his eyes.

"Do you have a boyfriend who is looking at us?" he asked somewhat sarcastically.

"That's not really important. However, listen to me. Maybe you can help me."

He seemed somehow surprised by my serious voice.

"Surely, definitely yes."

We continued to dance as I told him about everything that had happened to me.

"Maybe you can help me. If you can't yourself, you may tell my story to my uncle. His name is P.D. He is directly in charge of Education and Culture."

As soon as he heard my uncle's name, he became more serious and said, "I did not know this."

"Why, what did you know then?"

"Let's go and sit," he said. And we sat down at the nearest table.

"This is actually why I have come here," he continued. "They have made your problem a big deal, and that's why they sent me immediately here to find out the truth."

"What?" I asked, surprised again. "My problem at the committee? But I haven't done anything at all. The truth is that others only exaggerated."

"I know," he said, "it is a matter of rules and discipline." He lowered his voice. "This state power is very strong. Coming closer to me, he whispered into my ear, "They can't do anything to you. You are the niece of P.D. He is the head of that Committee."

But I have done nothing." I said this very nervously, not understanding what all this mess was about.

"I know, I know," he repeated. "But this state power is a communist power. It exercises the class struggle, and tries to suppress any ideas of the youth. It keeps the people in poverty and ignorance. But just for telling you these things, I might end up in prison." Suddenly his expression hardened, appeared more manly.

"This Party will not last much longer, but you have to be very careful. All those who are members of the Communist Party, or work for that Party in power, are living the last days of this regime. You hear me? I believe, when the time comes, we all, the youth, must overthrow this system. Democracy must be established here as in the rest of the world."

"But you still work for them?" I said, surprised.

"True, this is true, but I don't like their ideas. I like freedom of speech and action. I want to go wherever I want. You understand what I mean?"

He was speaking in a low voice again.

"Please, do not tell anyone what we discussed together. It is very dangerous. You are a very smart girl. Okay? You hear me?"

I was feeling strangely confused in my mind, partly from the music and partly because I was not understanding what was happening.

"Please, I am kindly asking your permission to leave now!"

While talking to him, I was looking for Arbi. There he was. Our eyes crossed again. He bowed his head to me and raised it again. The youth secretary understood that I was looking at Arbi, giving him the impression that I was asking for help. He left saying,

"We'll meet again. Goodbye, and stay strong!"

After a while I saw him sitting with Arbi. Perhaps he was chatting about the same things. The music stopped for some minutes. The school principal went to the platform close to the music band. I don't remember anything he said. I was already lost in nowhere.

"Long live the Communist Party!" the principal yelled at the end of his speech. Applause followed in the hall.

The emcee announced, "Dancing may continue! Girls have the power!"

But girls were not moving. Boys waited for a while and, when they saw that nothing was happening, took over the initiative for dancing again. Arbi did not move or try to approach me. I was sure he had received strict orders. All this was torture. I impatiently waited for that party to end. I could not stand it anymore. Finally I stood up and left for the third floor where we were supposed to sleep.

"Where are you going?" asked that beast, the dorm guardian. Her voice was harsh.

"To the room. I am so tired," I answered with the same harsh tone.

"Listen here! You better stop talking back to me in that tone! I'll show you better tomorrow when we are back at school. I did inform your parents, too. So you can't escape it." She was saying these words clenching her teeth in anger. She grabbed my arm and was squeezing it forcibly.

"Release my arm," I shouted at her wildly. "What kind of mother are you? What kind of guardian are you who exercises violence against young girls?"

"Shut up," she yelled aggressively. Music stopped. But she had lost her mind, "Let's see who is going to win, you or me! I am a member of the Communist Party, and, for the sake of its ideals, I will break your bones." Her yelling was interrupted by the crowd of students who did not at all like her wild voice.

The students in the hallway yelled, "Ooo - and boo!" This brought a hint of a smile to my face and it felt good that the students were supporting me. Together with them, there were some teachers, too, siding with us. I did not speak, but within me I felt somehow safer. I made three steps to the door and turned back. Came closer to her ear and whispered, "This will be your end."

She crossed her eyes in fury, and said, "I can't believe it! I can't believe all this!"

As soon as she left the hall muttering to herself, music started again. I cast my eyes over the hall again where all the students were dancing carefree. I also saw many faces looking at me. Among them was he, my love. My hand went a little up as if to say good night. I made a few steps toward the door. Only after the third step I heard his lovely voice say, "Wait a little!" Arbi's hand stretched out and, without speaking, he held my hand and pulled me away. I did not ask him, but followed, looking at him in the eyes. He was walking backwards. All started to shout out, "Bravo! Yes, yes! Good for you!" And the conductor of the music band chose to conduct a well-known romantic tune. The students made a big circle.

"Ready?" whispered Arbi into my ear. I made the yes-sign with my head. Without understanding, I began to follow Arbi's steps and the sweet romantic music. I felt myself a princess. While dancing, Arbi whispered again, "They can't stop us." His hands held my hands tightly. I rested my head on his chest, very touched by all what was happening. Tears rolled down my chin.

"Everything will be fixed," he said again. "Let's go. I'll accompany you to the room."

While leaving the hall we saw the beast in the opposite room. She was in discussion with one of her colleagues very angrily. It seemed that her colleague was defending us.

"Now I remember," I said to Arbi. "He is somehow different. He was at the same table with us on the train. Do you remember him?"

"Oh, yes. I remember him. He seems wiser, more relaxed."

They stared at us for some seconds. And, by the way she looked, we could read it in her eyes: *You see! They make love openly. This has never been seen or heard of.*

We walked to the room and stopped in front of the door.

"They ordered me not to be around you anymore. I don't know what decision they will make when we return to school. You have to excuse me for everything." Then he hugged me with all his strength.

I said, "Someone came and spoke with me tonight at the dancing party. He was the Youth Secretary for the whole district. But he seemed to be very courageous. He spoke about the new revolution and about overthrowing the communist regime. He showed me what democracy means."

"Shush, even the walls have got ears here," whispered Arbi. "I know all. He is talking to many other students about this. Therefore be very careful, okay? You talk to your parents tomorrow and tell them the truth. Whatever happens, I will be on your side. Okay, do you agree?" He was talking quickly. "Do you hear me?" he stressed again, touching my eyebrows. He used to do this often. Then he pretended to fix my bangs. But within me I knew that this was one of his gestures when he was nervous.

"Okay," I said, a little tired and surprised at the same time. It was more than I had thought. It seemed like a true revolution. Was I part of that revolution, too? I didn't know what was coming next. I was exhausted and, whatever the case, it was impossible to discover the answers to all the questions that were burning in my mind, I rested my head once more on Arbi's chest, who seemed to have understood everything.

"You seem very tired. Go and sleep now! I am sure you will feel better tomorrow." He said these words, continuing to caress my cheeks and chin. Of course, I didn't dare stop him from doing this.

"Good night, then!" I said, looking straight into his eyes.

"No kisses at all?" he said and didn't wait. "Good night, my princess!"

"Good night, my dear!"

"Good night.... and each "good night" was followed by a hot kiss. Oh, how I loved those kisses! And, while kissing each other, I took two steps back and was resting against the door of the room. How much I wanted to invite him inside during those moments! I knew that other girls would return after a while from the dancing party. I did not think long. I pushed the door with my back saying, "Come on in! I want to ..." before finishing my word, his finger stopped my lips.

"Shush...." he said with a burning whisper. Not waiting any longer he lifted me in his arms, kissing me like crazy. We struck something accidentally, but did not feel any pain. He threw me on the first nearest bed and continued to kiss each part of my body. Stopped for a moment and said, "Are you okay?"

Me, fearing that he might interrupt what he had started, shook my head as a sign of approval. We felt very close to each other and not only physically; all our feelings were melded into one. I could see this in his eyes and in everything he was saying or doing.

"Do you feel better now?" he asked, as the kisses and hugs relaxed him. I looked into his eyes and shook my head as a sign of approval.

"When I am with you, I forget everything else," I said smiling.

"I feel good for that," he replied with all sweetness.

"I'd better go now. You go to sleep and we talk tomorrow, okay?" He said this and kissed my hair. I stood up to accompany him to the door, still not speaking. I felt my mouth locked.

"Okay?" he asked again.

Okay, okay," I said, letting him understand that I was not ready to let him go.

"I know that you are upset tonight," he continued, "but you will understand me later. Good-night!"

"Goodnight," I said as well, and watched him walk away down the long corridor.

I shouldn't have but perhaps I was expecting too much from Arbi. I wished he stayed longer with me. But he always proved to be more rational. After he left I turned the light off and threw myself under the sheets of my bed, thinking about what might happen next day.

When the girls came in, I was still awake, though my eyes were closed.

I listened to their different comments, like: "that boy danced beautifully, or your dress fit you nicely, or oh, I feel pain in my feet…."

I was smiling to myself about the very natural discussion of the moment. While they continued their comments, I felt my eyelids grow heavier….

Next morning we dressed quickly, grabbed the bags we had made ready earlier, and ran to the train station. All had gathered there. I did not separate from other girls for a second, though I didn't speak at all. On the train I sat with the same girls next to me. To my surprise, Arbi did not come to sit with me. Instead of him the boy who was older than us joined us.

"May I sit here?" he asked.

"Yes, definitely," answered the other girls very pleased.

"For a long trip like this you need to have company," he continued. Then, just as if he knew what I was thinking, he said, "Arbi cannot sit near you. They have ordered him not to do so."

I did not say anything and interrupted him quickly.

"I know," he said, "but your eyes speak it clearly. You have it written here," and pointed to my forehead.

The girls laughed loudly. I felt good somehow, too, hearing his words, but didn't show it off.

"There you are," he said again. "You look very beautiful when you smile."

"Stop with this nonsense," I told him, turning my eyes to the window.

The train had already started to move. I was looking at the endless green fields. Here and there you could see people working in those fields. I felt some kind of sadness.

"What are you thinking?" asked a friend in front of me.

"Many things," I said. "I don't know what to tell my parents. Neither do I know what I have done. I don't know why it has become so seemingly tragic."

"Listen here," said the boy who was sitting next to me. "I work for them. They are feeling the fear in their bones. They feel the changes taking place so fast, and are trying to stop the new times that are coming. They try to suppress everything that goes against this communist system. And they have it easier to rule over the ignorant people, but now they can't do anything to us - the youth. We are those who have to overthrow the regime once and for all. Democracy, only democracy, will make it possible for us to achieve our dreams." He was speaking very passionately.

"Ema, would you like to be engaged as you already are now, or be free to freely express your love for Arbi?"

"I am trying, but ...." I said after listening to him attentively.

"I know," he said, not letting me finish my word. "But they don't allow you to do that. In a way they are scared by the reality now."

"It seems that he is falling in love with you," said Irena, the girl sitting face to face with the Youth Secretary. He laughed and, feeling no embarrassment, said, "I am not surprised. I am like honey and can stick anywhere or to anybody." We all laughed at his joke.

The travel was going well. The boy never stopped talking and giving instructions all the way back. There were moments when he moved to other tables. Though the travel was coming to an end, I hadn't seen Arbi yet. Perhaps he was at the other end in the train. When we disembarked from the train, I tried to look for him again but saw him nowhere. Tired of the trip and of searching for him, I turned around to continue walking to the dormitory together with others.

While walking, a hand touched me slightly and a low voice whispered to me, "Here, you have a letter from Arbi." She gave me the folded letter and left in a hurry. I did not open it, deciding to open and read it quietly in my room. I hurried and in a few minutes threw my book-bag on the ground. I could not wait and began reading the letter:

"Dear Ema! I apologize for everything that happened. I would want things to be different. They gave me the order not to approach you. I am not allowed to speak to you. Such a love as ours has a negative effect on others. That's what they told me. I don't know what will happen next. But I only know one thing: You will forever be in my heart. I will always love you, wherever you may be! Sincerely, A"

"What else is left to be done against me now?" I said to myself, and crumpled the letter in my fist. "I hate all this control everywhere! I hate all and everything!" I shouted.

"You'd better stop it, idiot! They will hear you," said Eli, grabbing the letter from my hand and reading it. "You don't have to worry about this. Go and meet your parents. They are in the principal's office."

Good gracious! That bitch had given the alarm. How could I explain to them that I had done nothing? I only was in love with a boy.

This was my crime. Coming closer, I saw the principal explaining something and moving his hand. They were in front of him. By their side stood my tutelary teacher and the bitch. As soon as they saw me, they all stood up as if bitten by a snake. My mother came close and said, "What is all this disgrace, my daughter?" She had tears in her eyes. Father did not say anything at all. He looked at me with remorse.

"Sit here," said the principal, a respected person in the school. "Now tell us! What has happened?" He leaned back, resting his arms on the table.

"Nothing," I said, with a courage of a crazy woman. "But this dorm guardian fabricates and exaggerates things. She has also beaten me up vigorously. And I am neither the first, nor the last. She treats all the girls this same way." After I finished, I waited to receive a positive reply. The principal did not speak. The dorm guardian goggled her eyes and said, "You see, she is arrogant. She is supercilious and above all she has new ideas that she wants to introduce to other girls. For this I request she be expelled from dormitory and school." While she was speaking in a point-blank voice, her hand hammered the table angrily. The principal noticed that and said, "You are responsible for the dormitory, but for the school we are responsible." At that moment the Youth Secretary entered the office. Surely they all knew he was sent by the Central Committee.

"Greetings," he said, and, before anyone else spoke, he started, "I have come as a representative for all the youth of this city and the Central Committee has sent me here for just this problem. This student has done nothing. She is a student with excellent academic achievement. The only crime for which she has been accused is that she expresses openly her love for a boy. If all of you think that this is a crime or an unacceptable new idea, then we, the youth, would oppose it. And here you have the signature of the chairman of Education and Culture. He continued to read some papers and, when he read the name of the chairman of Education and Culture, the principal noticed that his last name was the same as mine.

Surprised by this, the principal asked, "What relation do you have to this person?"

"He is my uncle," I answered proudly.

-"Ahaa! Okay." Then he added, "You may go out and wait! We'll make the decision."

I went out, expecting that my parents would follow me. They did not. Instead, after some minutes, the Youth Secretary came out. Now I was feeling even more respect for him.

"Thank you," I said to him with a smile.

"I did what I could," he said. "It depends on them now."

"I know, but I don't understand why you are helping me."

"Because I support the new ideas, and want to help bring democracy to this country."

"Be careful," I told him in a low voice. "If they hear this you will end in prison."

"It is even worth dying for it if we make the change the whole youth movement is wanting now. Long live democracy!" Then, shaking hands with me as a sign of respect, he said goodbye. What a courageous person! He was right there in the middle of that communist party yet was working to overthrow that regime. We all knew how strict and almost impossible it was to make any progress at all. And none dared rebel against it. All those who had tried to say something, were sentenced to death. Therefore this young man seemed great to me. My thoughts were interrupted by the school principal, who motioned to me

- "Come and hear the decision we have made!"

I went in and sat next to my parents.

"Okay," started the school principal. "From today on you are expelled from the dormitory, but you are allowed to graduate school. This was our decision. One more little mistake and you may be expelled from school."

I was satisfied with this decision. In fact I hated to return to that dormitory where girls were treated like nuns. Without being ashamed at all, and with the courage of a crazy person, I said, "What decision did you make about the dormitory guardian who unjustly tortures the girls?"

To my surprise, the principal said, "We'll discuss it in the next meeting. Please, you are free and may leave now."

"Let's go," said father, not looking me in the eyes. We went out and stopped somewhere at the corner of the schoolyard where no people were around.

"Do you know that you have discredited us? What are these things I am hearing? You are an engaged girl. Today, even right now, you will come home and we will marry you to the one to whom you are engaged! Do you hear me? I did not give you the opportunity to attend school to discredit us. What is all this? Tell me!"

I had never before seen my father so angry.

"They will fire me," he continued, "because my daughter has new political ideas. And not only that. You have stained my reputation with infamy for the rest of my life. You, my daughter, by breaking the rules and moral customs."

"But I...." I could not finish the sentence.

"That's enough! I don't want any discussion! It has never been heard of or seen that a daughter opposes her father, and much worse, to love someone when she is already engaged. What shall I say to your fiance? That my daughter is not for you? Oh God! What a shame!"

"I don't care for him at all. I am sorry that you do not understand me." I was speaking with tears in my eyes and full of anger. My mother was not speaking.

"Close your mouth!" said father, putting the hand on his heart. "You will come to the village right now! There is no school for you anymore! Tomorrow I will fix the day of marriage." His last words were stated like a command. I was terribly scared by that decision.

"Please father, allow me to finish school. I'll stop all connections and will only care about my lessons. Please! After I finish school you decide anything you want. Please!" I began crying.

"On one condition," said father after a pause. "We fix the date for the marriage now."

I did not speak. Everything was over for me because whatever I said would be useless. I would oppose him in vain. Nobody in the world could go against him in that moment.

"Take whatever you have to from the dorm and let's go! We'll send you to your uncle until you finish school. I can't let you go back and forth on the buses. That would give you chances to meet 'your beloved boy'. Finish school and then marry the man to whom you are engaged. Otherwise you will never return to your family."

After hearing this my heart was utterly worn out. I ran away crying and kept doing so while collecting my things in the room.

"Don't worry at all," one of my roommates said, trying to calm me. "We will see you in school."

When I was leaving I saw that bitch of the school dormitory at the main entrance.

"Goodbye," she said in a self-satisfied voice, by which she meant to say: *you see what I can do to you?*

I breathed deeply, smiled, and said, "We'll see. This world is round. Whatever you try to do, I am going to graduate school. And I promise that when I graduate, I am going to come and show you my diploma." After saying this, I left, imagining her trying to stare me down. I returned to my parents.

"Let's go," said mother. Father walked ahead of us. Me and my mother walked silently. When we entered my uncle's house, we noticed the smell of cooked fish. We all ate without talking much. My father was talking to the uncle about work. My problems were not touched on at all. After dinner my uncle joined me and said, "You are a smart girl. We're going to understand each other."

"Yes," I affirmed.

"Great! Bravo! Let me arrange the rest. Go now! Sleep and rest! Tomorrow will be a new day."

They stayed on long after I went to bed. Next morning my parents were gone. I got ready for school and said goodbye to my uncle and his wife, who were drinking their morning coffee.

"Wait," said my uncle. "I'll come with you today. I want to talk to the principal."

And so we did. When we arrived, my uncle entered the principal's office and I went to my class. No one asked me anything. I did not see Arbi. They had sent him to the other parallel class. If he dared speak to me, he would be expelled from school. After what had happened, I lost my courage and only continued to study like an idiot just trying to forget everything else.

Many days passed without any specially interesting event. I was only hoping to get some news from Arbi, but this didn't happen either. He had received strict orders. Or, after all we had gone through, perhaps he had given in. Weeks were rolling on and the end of the school year was coming.

Finally, exam time came. All were terribly scared. I used to hear this from my girlfriends. These exam results would affect the grades of the whole school year. I wasn't in the mood to study at all. I just kept saying to myself: *what I have already learned is enough. Let come what may! I don't care!* When I went in for the first exam, I saw Arbi sitting at one of the desks. There were some other students, too. Three teachers were in front of us. A few minutes after we started the exam, I felt that the dormitory tutelary was behind me. It seemed that she had been advised by my uncle to help me. I understood this because he came next to me and said, "Do you need help?"

"No, but can you please go and help him over there?" I pointed out at Arbi, who seemed to be somehow lost. My request was denied.

I finished soon and handed my exam papers over to the teacher at the table. They asked me a few other oral questions, which actually seemed easy for me and I tried to answer them carefully. There were some political questions, as well, taken from the book called Marxism. Those questions were not easy to understand, but I had somehow studied and learned them by heart. One question only was provocative. "What would you do if somebody broke the rules the Albanian Communist Party has taught us?"

I thought a little and quietly said, "My father is member of this party. He has taught me that when someone falls into a pit, you must give him a hand to lift him up and not kick him down deeper into that pit."

My answer was unclear to them, but apparently they saw nothing to censor. Arbi raised his head and made a sign with his finger - good!

Then I went into the classroom. The other exams were easier. After some days we were done with them. They displayed the list with exam grades at the class window. I ran to find out my results.

There I read: 7, 9, 9. The highest grade you could get was 10. I had got 7 in politics, or what then was called Marxism. After that I carefully searched for names starting with letter A. After some other A-names, I found Arbi's name with grades 6, 7, 6. At least, and most important is he had passed the classes. Somehow satisfied and with a smile on my face, I left for my uncle's home. At last we had managed to finish the year without catastrophe. What would happen next I didn't know.

In the meantime I would wait anxiously to see Arbi. Now nobody could stop us from making our plans. Now I could meet him without any concerns and no one could tell me that I was breaking school rules. I could even go and live with Arbi if he agreed to that. With these thoughts in mind I walked down the road leading to my uncle's neighborhood, though I didn't want to return home before seeing Arbi. I heard a familiar tone a few steps behind. It made my heart beat faster. Should I turn my head or not? The music stopped. I kept walking without turning my head yet. A strong anxiety was pinching me inside.

Who could be a few steps behind me? And that familiar music? And there, the music started again. I did not wait anymore. I turned my head around. I didn't believe my eyes. It was Arbi. But I tried to restrain myself.

"Hey, is it really you?"

"Why? Are you waiting for someone else?" he said with a light smile.

"Maybe," I answered.

"It seems you are still angry with me. I know I haven't spoken to you for quite a long time now." He said it with some nervousness. "But you must know that I was not allowed. We both would have been expelled. Understand?"

He continued to walk very close to me.

I knew this was true and did not argue. I put my arm under his, and, leaning against him, continued walking ahead, not caring where we were going.

He liked it. "I have missed you."

I looked him in the eyes. "Indeed?" I teased him.

"Yes much," he continued with a soft voice, and kissed me gently on the forehead.

"Let's go to the park," I said, but I only have one hour. If I am late, my uncle will be concerned."

"Let's go then. We shouldn't waste time." He held my hand and started to run. We continued running and laughing for some minutes like two little children. The park was in the south end of the city. Beyond that park was the martyrs' cemetery. Close to it was a beautiful forest with olive trees. They looked to be in same distance from each other, and as it was a hill, the olive trees stood on terraces. Everything was really beautiful. From there you could see the whole city. I was looking somewhat bewildered by the beauty of the city, which I had never noticed until now. I turned to Arbi and said, "Isn't it beautiful? Why haven't I noticed it before, I wonder?"

"Because you have never been with me here," said Arbi with that very soft and appealing voice. "Besides that, what adds beauty to this place are the beloved couples of the city. Look around you!" I turned my head and saw couples here and there either kissing each other or leaning on each other and talking.

"How beautiful? Very beautiful, indeed," I said happily. Arbi came closer to me.

"You are very beautiful. You make this place even more beautiful." While talking, he had placed both his hands around my waist, and was looking straight into my eyes. "No one is going to separate us! No one!"

Oh, how happy I felt! I was looking at Arbi holding my head upward as he was rather tall and my lips were open. He bent over and gave me a light kiss.

"I love you much," he whispered to me. The next kiss was longer and deeper.

"I love you much, too, very much!" While speaking I kissed him like crazy on the lips, eyes, and neck.

"Let's sit somewhere!" I said, more relaxed after having expressed my feelings.

"I have never stopped thinking about you," said Arbi, holding my hands tight over his chest and kissing them. "At one point I thought I was losing you, but now you are mine."

Listening to these words I leaned even tighter against him.

"At last we succeeded," I said, kissing him lightly on the cheek.

"We still have another fight with the parents. Don't forget that you are engaged. They will not give up their concepts."

As he spoke, he kept kicking small pebbles with the heel of his shoe.

"Don't worry," I answered quickly without thinking. "I will continue my studies at the college. I don't want to marry. I am only eighteen years old now—not quite eighteen."

These discussions were making me nervous. Perhaps I knew that I would have it very difficult with my parents. Arbi understood this but he couldn't seem to help himself., "What would you think if you married me, then?"

I turned quickly to him and our eyes met. "Tonight?" I said without thinking.

He smiled, wrapped me in his arms and spun me in the air as if I were made of feathers. Then he put me on the ground and kissed me again.

"I would take you home tonight, but this would make you lose your parents for the rest of your life. You go home tomorrow and speak to them once more. If they don't change their mind, then I will leave it up to you."

I liked Arbi's mature thought. I hugged him and said, "I love you, love you, love...!" The last word drew the attention of others who turned their heads toward us. Arbi kissed me passionately, ignoring whoever was looking on.

"Let's go," he said. "I don't want you to hassle with your uncle."

So, hand in hand, we slowly left the park on the hill. At the end of the park I turned my head to Arbi and said, "Wait, if one day you miss me and want to see me, let me know to come here and it's where you'll find me, okay?"

"Okay," he answered, understanding that I had already lost my mind because of fear about what would happen next. We walked for a few minutes without speaking. When we arrived at the uncle's house, Arbi hugged me and said, "I will come tomorrow early in the morning. Go now and do not worry! Everything is going to work out."

Buoyed by Arbi's words, I ran down the steps leading to my uncle's apartment. At the end of the steps I gave Arbi a kiss by sign of my hand. He made the same sign in the air and put his hand over his heart.

As soon as I knocked on my uncle's door, it opened instantly.

"Where have you been, dear?" said uncle's wife. "We were worried about you."

I ate dinner very quietly and after that helped wash dishes in the kitchen. Suddenly a knock was heard on the door. I turned my head and asked, "Are you expecting anybody at this hour?"

"It should be your father," answered my uncle and hurried to open the door. Yes, it was my parents, indeed. My mother was holding a stewing pot with something roasted in it which smelled good. No doubt, this was done as a sign of gratitude to my uncle who had cared for me.

"I was told that you had good results in last exams," my father said.

"Somehow I did well," I answered proudly. "Why did you come so late?" I asked my mother.

"Eh, my daughter, we better speak at our home about it," said mother in a low voice.

"What has happened?" I asked again with curiosity.

"We'll make a big wedding," said father. "In two weeks, starting from today, we'll have the wedding. Yesterday we fixed the date with our new friends."

These words coming straight from my father's mouth struck me deep in my heart. I had already forgotten what would happen after I finished school. I had already forgotten him, my fiance. My uncle kept his eyes down to avoid looking me in the eyes."

"Listen to me!" I said very angry. "I will not marry a man I don't know at all. I am in love with someone else. You know this very well. He is someone who understands me. Someone who has got progressive ideas about today's life. And above all, he shares the same ideas with me. Therefore don't even think that I am going to marry somebody else."

All were standing there with their mouths open as if terrible things were coming out of my mouth. And I don't know how I got all that courage to oppose them. None spoke for the moment. While I was waiting for my father to scream out and say: stop, or zip your mouth! to my surprise, he asked, "What are these new ideas that you and he, your lover, have? Can you explain it for us?"

I smiled grimly and said, "Oh, my God! How many ideas we have! Here are some of them: how to help the youth movement to overthrow this communist regime; to get rid of the old traditions and customs that destroy young girls' lives by marrying them forcibly. We want to bring freedom of speech and press, free to speak in peace, to be allowed to attend church, and many, many more things that communism opposes. We want to live in democracy."

My father, very angry, interrupted me:

"Democracy? You want to overthrow that power I am working for? But you know, I am a member of that party. It has never been seen or heard of that your daughter fights you, or is against you! And you know well that I will end directly in prison just for these ideas you have in your head. You know that your whole family: your mother, your sisters, and your brother, because of these ideas, will be deported somewhere in the remotest parts of the country. And your uncle may be fired because of these idiot ideas. Communism has got a very strong grip on class struggle policy. This would destroy all of us. Do you understand, or not?" At this moment father yelled at the top of his voice and put his hand over his heart.

I did not speak. I noticed that around his dry mouth were traces of white foam, maybe due to the long speech. Then he seemed to be out of breath. I stood up and brought him a glass of water.

"Here you are, drink it!" I said it in a low voice.

"Tomorrow... will... will go... ho...me and you will marry.... Don't want to hear.... mo...r ....foo...lish...ness..s, and crap."

These were his last words. He fell from the chair, and we tried to keep him from hitting the cement floor. We put a pillow under his head. Mother was shouting, "You see what you did to us, my daughter! One day you will kill all of us."

"We must send him to the hospital," said the uncle. "Otherwise he is going to die in our hands. You stay here," he ordered me.

I obeyed. I was scared to death. My uncle's wife went to the neighbors to ask for help. Two men came quickly, and, together with my uncle, sent father to a hospital. My mother did not speak anymore, though tears continued. When all had left, I felt terribly sad. I remembered the words of my mother: you will kill all of us. I didn't know what to do. I was almost out of breath and choking. I sat in the middle of that empty room and started to pray, "Please God ! Please, save my father from death! I will do anything he will say to me. Please!"

My words were fading away because of the anguish I was going through. The fear that my father was dying because of me, terrified me. I kept weeping and murmuring to myself until I fell asleep. Next morning I woke up early when I heard the outer door opened and closed forcibly. I got up immediately and asked what had happened. My uncle's wife had just returned from the hospital.

"They put him in the operation hall," she said, sitting on a chair in the kitchen, looking very tired. "He is still in there,"

I threw myself into her arms, crying.

"That's enough now," she said to me, trying to make me pull myself together.

"You dress up and go to see him…if you want."

I dressed quickly, blew my nose, dried my tears, and went out. The day seemed rather cold to me, though temperatures were not so low. I was shaking all over. Hurrying to the hospital, I entered and asked where my father was. The nurse looked at me as if to say, "What do you want here? You are the reason why your father is dying."

"Room thirteen," she said in a heavy tone. "On the left."

"Thank you," I said in my low voice, and continued in that direction. I stopped at door number 13. I heard my mother's voice, "So much time has already passed. What is going on?"

"I just came out from the operation room. They are almost done." This was my uncle's voice.

I did not go in. Instead, I looked for the operation room. I don't know, but I felt that I wasn't strong enough to look my mother or uncle straight in the face. I was feeling guilty indeed, without understanding why. Walking through the corridor leading to the operation hall, I heard steps and voices. Two doctors were talking to each other, "He survived this time, but his heart is very weak. He cannot resist strong emotions," said one of the doctors. "I think he has to start exercises and switch off his mind from any concerns if he wants to live a few more years," said a younger doctor, removing his apron. While talking, they had come rather close to me.

"May we help you?" the younger doctor asked me.

"I am here to see my father," I said and two teardrops ran down my cheeks. "I am his daughter."

"We are very happy to tell you that your father is out of danger."

"Thank you so much. May I see him now?"

"Well, give him some two hours, at least," said the younger doctor. "But you may see him through the window."

"Thank you," I said, walking in that direction.

"You're welcome, one said, and added,

"We will inform your mother about this good news."

I continued to the operation hall. The window was quite wide and allowed me to see everything inside.

There I glimpsed my father lying on the bed, covered with white sheets. Some tubes were attached to his mouth and other parts of his body.

Good heavens! My eyes went wide due to the fear of what I was seeing now, and of the thought that everything happened because of me. I felt shortness of breath, pain in the stomach and nausea. I ran quickly to the nearest restroom. After cleaning myself and freshening up with cold water, I looked at myself in the mirror. My face was still pale.

"Do you understand that you are killing your father with your own hands?" I said to myself in a loud voice, staring at my image in the mirror. "You are thinking only of yourself. Shame on you!" I was angry.

Closing my eyes for a moment a decision came to my mind. It was a harsh ice-cold decision: marry that man your parents chose for you. Make this sacrifice if you want your father to live. This inner voice was blunt and unchangeable. Very blunt!

I left the restroom aimlessly, not knowing where my feet were sending me. I made my way out of hospital. I felt the fresh air on my face. I felt cold, very cold. My whole body was shaking while I continued back to my uncle's house. While walking I felt people's shoulders brush against me. I would repeatedly hear voices saying, "Watch your step, girl!"

I was looking at nowhere, just somewhere far away, still not knowing where. Suddenly I realized I was passing the steps of the school building. And right there, sitting like a statue, I saw Arbi. Without saying a word, I sat next to him. I rested my head on him and started to cry.

After having learned what happened, Arbi did not speak for these moments either. Instead, he grabbed me by the shoulders and held me tight. We stayed like that for a bit.

"Everything will be fixed," he said with regret. I turned my head immediately.

"Will be fixed? My father is dying! Do you understand that? And it's because of me, his daughter, who has got new ideas about life. Me, his daughter, who thinks only about herself. Understand? It is me who is the cause he is dying." My hands were shaking as I spoke. And tears again were surely making their way down the cheeks.

"I am an idiot! An idiot!" I breathed deeply with eyes closed.

"That's not true, not true at all! We all are doing the same thing," said Arbi with a soft voice. "It just happened that your father is not in good health. Everything will be fixed. Make up your mind! Let's go and have a warm tea! Come on!" He pulled me by the arm, and gave me a light kiss on my forehead.

"No, thank you." I jumped up for fear that I might change the decision I had already made. "Please, stay away! I have made a decision. I will marry the man I don't know and don't love. Everything is already done now. Please, you must stay away from me!"

I stood up to go inside because I did not want to see his eyes. He stood in my way and shouted, "No, now you are making a mistake! You hear me? I love you, love you!"

"That's enough! Go now," I said in a softer voice. I did not raise my head. He understood.

"You are not looking me in the eyes. Look me in the eyes and tell me to go."

I looked up. His eyes were wet and red. His face was splotchy. His lower lip was quivering. I kissed him passionately and violently. "Go now! I have made the decision. Go and live your life! Think no more of me, ever! Live your life!"

I left him there and went toward my uncle's home.

"No, no!" I heard from behind. I entered and slammed the door behind me. I could not hear any more. Perhaps I was not strong enough to see and hear that reality. Alone in the room I kept crying. It felt like I was choking. My tears were drying up. The whole room was spinning. It seemed like the whole world was collapsing. I covered my head with the pillow. I don't know how long I kept crying like that. Next morning I got up and prepared everything before leaving for the village. When I was zipping up the traveling-bag, the door opened. I saw my mother, the uncle, and my aunt. All seemed tired. My uncle approached me and said, "Father is out of danger."

His words were followed by a smile and he stretched his arms to me. I threw myself in his arms. Then I hugged my mother, telling her, "Everything will be okay. I will do whatever father says."

"Okay, my daughter!" she said and added, "So was it meant, my daughter, so was it."

My uncle was smoking and I saw the spreading curls of smoke rising from his pipe. He did not speak. Only shook his head as a sign of approval. After a little rest, mother and the others went to the kitchen and spoke in low voices.

"Are you ready?" asked mother. "We have to go now. The uncle will take care of your father. They will come together to the village."

And so it happened. We left, and after some days I saw my uncle coming from the hospital holding my father by his arm. My sisters and the brother ran to hug him. Father hugged them all, saying, "I love you much, much."

I was already frozen like a statue just two steps away from him. He raised his head and said, "What do you say? Will we make the wedding, or not?"

"Whatever you say, father. I am glad that you are well. Everything will be done just as you want it."

- "That is so, my daughter, very good."

From that moment everything took a downward turn, rolling down very fast. Each day I would see aunts, mother's sister, cousins, friends of the family, all helping prepare for the day of wedding. I stayed locked in my room. I was completely numb and felt like a thunderstruck creature. One of my aunts would repeatedly come to my room. She did put some kind of mask on my face. I did not refuse anything.

"Today we received the new white bridal dress," she said. "Now you have to try it on!"

I did not speak. I stared through the window, instead. My imagination was lost somewhere far - far away.

"Come over here! Take off that blouse!" And, not waiting for me to do that, she took my loose blouse off. "Come on now! Put this on. Wow! My aunt's soul! How beautiful you look! You are your aunt's star, indeed."

After I had put the white dress on, according to tradition, the whole family should come to the room to see me, the bride, dressed. Aunt opened the door and said, "Ready, you may come in!"

The first to enter were my sisters. On their faces I noticed both surprise and smiles. But the elder sister did not approach me. As soon as she saw me, she burst into tears and turned around to avoid me seeing her like that. Whereas all the others, like aunts, mother's sisters and family friends stood around me congratulating my parents and eating the caramels served on this occasion. I knew why my elder sister was crying. She very well understood my pain. She had suffered the same thing before me.

Three days were left before the wedding day. My aunt, who was taking care of me, said, "I have arranged all your gifts. They are not much--still good, not bad. On Wednesday we will do your hair because the whole village will come to see how the bride looks. Do you hear me?"

"I hate everything!" I said in a throttled voice because of the anguish I was living through at this moment.

"Shush... don't speak like that! Come on, you're your aunt's soul! Aunt's star! All will go well. Shall I bring you something to eat, dear? You look like your belly has shrunken to the bones. What is it you want? Do you want to make all of us sick?"

"I wish I were dead," I said.

She raised her head. "Make up your mind! You saw what you did to your father with your freakish acts. Come on! Let it be the last time I hear such complaints from you! I love you so much, my soul!" She continued patting my face with her hand.

Very angry, I stood up and spoke, "Okay. You are younger than my parents. Perhaps you understand me better. How can I be happy when I don't love that person I have to marry? Secondly, what will happen to me in an unknown family? Surely I will become a little woman who will only cook and clean for his whole family--ordered by others to obey them all the time. Will it not be so? Tell me the truth now! You know well, my aunt, that I have so many dreams in my head, and, together with my friends and other people, we are trying to build up a new world–the democracy, where all people are free to speak, to choose their own life without being forced by others. That's who I am."

It was obvious that the loud discussion with my aunt had been heard in the other room because my sister hurried in and said, "Stop! You are being heard even out in the street. Come on, my soul! Calm down!" She continued touching me on the shoulders. "Tonight the whole youth of the village will come to say goodbye to you."

"Indeed?!" I asked, surprised.

"Yes, yes, at six p.m. And you should have your new white dress on for this occasion. At noon we will do your hair. Everything is going to work well. You will see! Okay?" she asked me, watching my face so that I wouldn't do any insane thing at the last moment.

I looked her straight in her eyes and asked her, "Do I have any other choice when our father is sick?"

"No," she said, "but have it clear in your mind that everything is going to work well. What do you say, my soul?"

The thought that I was going to meet my friends for the last time did not leave my mind for a second. Would they judge me for having accepted this marriage? Nevertheless, I was going to see once more those faces so dear to me. Maybe not.... No, no, it is not possible. And, maybe he doesn't want to see me anymore. A strange thought passed through my mind – Arbi ! What was he doing right now?

The time came. It was 6:00 p.m. and I was ready, waiting in anxiety to be taken away from the room. After some minutes my elder sister came into my room and said, "Are you ready? They have come." I breathed deeply and said, "Okay, okay." My sister opened the door. Oh! My God! I heard those voices so dear and well-known to me.

"Wow, how beautiful you have become! And your hair has grown so much!"

I saw their faces one by one.

"Oh! How much I have missed you!" I said at last and hugged them one by one. All surrounded me but no one was talking.

"I know," I said, "that you may have many questions. But ...." I did not finish my words. From the end of the group the Youth Secretary spoke, "We know everything," and he was stressing it in a convinced tone. "How is the father now?"

"Not so good," I said somehow quieter.

"We want to wish you a happy life," he said. "We'll be on your side in everything. We'll continue our fight for freedom and democracy, and on your behalf, too."

"Absolutely! We will do so," other voices in the group agreed. My heart was filling with joy. I looked down for a moment and then asked, "What's going on with Arbi? Has anyone of you seen him?"

Absolute silence. Hot tears ran down my cheeks as soon as I mentioned his name.

"I don't understand; why is this silence! What has happened?" I asked, frightened.

"Oh, no, no, nothing," spoke Dita, coming closer to me.

"Then, why do all of you have tears in your eyes? Why?"

"Because we know how much you loved each other. We feel very sorry," she said, and could not hide her feelings. "But you know how strong he is. Me and all others stay close to him. Do not worry at all," said Dita, wiping her tears with a napkin and leaving some black stains from her make-up. "What shall I do? He doesn't care at all about me," she said and laughed loudly. We all laughed. I held Dita's hands and told her, "Take care of him, please!"

"Okay, I promise you," she said, embracing me again.

"What about us over here? Are we allowed to hug the bride?" said the humorist of the class.

I looked at him for a second and opened my arms without answering him.

"I have never seen a more beautiful bride," he whispered, while embracing me. I hugged all the rest with respect and love. I had a feeling as if I was going to die. As if I would never see them again, and I kept crying the whole time I was with them. At the last moment I saw the Youth Secretary putting a package next to me. He kissed my hand and said,

"May you have a happy life! This is for you from all of us together."

I opened the package and saw in it a very beautiful gift. It was an album with photos from all of us together taken at different times during our school years. This was the most precious gift they could have given. I held it tight over my heart, saying,

"I will never forget you, never!"

We hugged again before they left.

"Do not forget, our country will change soon." These were last words by the Youth Secretary.

Remaining alone in the room, I quickly opened the album I had kept in my hands the whole time. On the first page were all the graduates who had studied from 1982 to 1986, three parallel classes together. I looked at all of them one by one. Here is me! On my left was Lili and on the right was Dita. Behind me, Arbi. Only a part of his body could be seen. I had not noticed that the day we made the picture he was right behind me. He was near me in most of the pictures. In the middle of the album there was an enlarged photo covering both pages. It was only me with him. A little note in handwriting was at the bottom of the photo: "Mine forever. Love You - Arbi." That was one of the photos we had made recently during the visit in the museum city.

I did not notice that the door was opened, and my father entered the room. His hand rested on my shoulder.

"How do you feel?" he asked me. I quickly closed the album and whispered, "Okay, how about you?" " "Up to now I feel good" he answered. "Listen, my daughter. I understand you and your ideas well. You can do whatever you want in the end. You and your friends may come out quite openly and say whatever you think. But have you ever thought of what will happen to you? I can tell you that. You and your friends will die in prisons. Your whole family and their families will end in the poorest zones of the country as deportees. That's what communism is. You speak, you are nipped in the bud." He raised his voice and put his hand over his heart as if he had pain again.

"Then why do you work for them if you don't like the regime?"

"Because I have six children and I want to feed them and make their life safe. This is why, you understand?" He said it, still keeping his hand over his heart.

I did not speak. Knowing that I could make him have another heart attack, I decided to say nothing. He kissed me on the forehead and went out groaning uh, huh, uh... That was a groaning I had been hearing often recently.

After the door closed, I went to the window to see what was going on in the front yard of the house. Cousins, both girls and boys, were entertaining and dancing different traditional dances of our country. The music kept going up and down both in sound and rhythm. People were coming and going. It was meaningless turmoil. This went on for a few days. At last Saturday came, the day when the wedding dinner would take place. All the invitees, according to the tradition, would bring a present or cash for the girl to be married. They would eat dinner and dance the whole night. In the morning only the close relatives of the family would stay, like uncles, the mother's and father's sisters, and cousins. All together would wait until the bridegroom would come to take the bride. That was the tradition. So it happened with me, too.

On Saturday evening, in my white dress, I stood in the middle of my parents at the main table. I felt all the glances of the wedding guests. I never raised my head at all. Just pretended to see something on the table. I only heard the noise of spoons and forks digging the food from dishes. For a while silence prevailed. I don't know why. Then I heard my uncle proposing the toast to all the guests.

"Cheers to all of you, my friends!"

"Cheeeeers!" the guests noisily replied.

"Tonight we are marrying our daughter. I wish her...." I did not pay any attention to what was happening. My eyes had caught a movement outside the circle of guests. Someone was over there in the darkness and had focused his eyes on me. I felt something like a burning in the stomach. Who might it be? Why was this person staying in the darkness?

"Do you hear or not?" my elder sister asked me. "The uncle is inviting you to stand up and drink a toast to all the guests."

Bewildered, I stood up, and glass in hand, walked slowly toward my uncle. Once again I turned my head to the man in the darkness. What if he was .....! Being completely absent-minded, I stumbled in the long white dress and almost fell on the floor. My uncle's wife, who was near me, held me and accompanied me to the table where my uncle was sitting. When I drew near him, I could not see the man in darkness again. He had disappeared. While all were ready to drink a toast to the bride's future, I was clicking my glass with others and kept thinking: maybe it was Arbi! Oh, Lord! And we were right in the middle of the dinner when suddenly everything became pitch dark. Lights went off. Something extraordinary.

I heard someone say, "Bring the bride inside! It may be a trick by that vagabond." My sister whispered into my ear, "It must be Arbi. He is making this mess in order to let you know that he is here. Come on inside," she told me, and tried to pull me forcibly.

"Wait," I said, "wait! What if he is here, here beside me?"

"Hey, you! Do come inside! Are you crazy? Phu...phu! You will discredit us!" She continued to speak and pulled me more forcibly again. We went inside the room.

"Sit and calm down now! I am going to get a candle," she said, leaving the room and poking her way through the darkness. To my surprise, the door closed.

"Who are you?" I asked, frightened.

"Who else would you like it to be?"

He had come very close to me. I knew that voice. I raised my hand and touched his face with my fingers. My whole being smiled.

"It's you?!" I shouted joyfully.

"Shush." He put his forefinger on my lip. We hugged each other like crazy. I don't know how long we stayed like that in each other's arms. Then he moved a step back, and said, "I could not help but see you once more. You will excuse me for the turmoil done. But all know of our love." While talking, he was holding my cheeks in his hands.

"I am sorry," I said, withdrawing from him. "You know that my heart will be forever with you, but I have no other choice."

"I heard what happened to your father. You have no reason to explain to me." He spoke, holding me with his arms around my waist. He came quite close to me. I felt his hot breath on my face. Our lips met, giving us both a real sweetness. A second kiss, another one.

"Take me with you," I spoke without thinking. "Let's go!"

He put his lips on my forehead and said, "You would not forgive yourself if something happened to your father. What do you say?"

I did not speak. We hugged again.

"I am completely destroyed spiritually, but I must do what is more logical for your sake. Do not cry!" He continued to speak to me, hearing my anguished moaning. He changed the topic. "You looked like a sylph there. I have never seen a more beautiful bride. While we talked the door of the room opened. My sister entered with a lit candle in hand.

"Gosh! You here! What do you want here? And why do you cry? What did he do to you?" she asked, very alarmed.

"Calm down," I told her. "He did nothing to me." Arbi did not move. "We are only talking" , I spoke again, while wiping tears in my eyes. "You must leave now," she insisted. "Was it not enough with the turmoil you created in our wedding? You left us in darkness, for God's sake!" Her threatening finger was dangling over his face. Still, respectfully, she withdrew her finger. He said, "I could not stand the idea of not seeing her. This is my bride. Mine!"

His eyes looked down and he turned slightly but it was obvious His eyes were wet and could not be hidden. The first tears rolled down his very manly face. My sister did not speak. Silence.

"Nevertheless you have to leave. You understand," said the sister, looking at him with regret.

"Yes," he said somehow quieter. "I'll leave."

"But, please, just let us alone for only a few minutes!" I asked my sister, touching her hand.

She went out saying, "When I come back I must not see you here!" The door closed. Under the candlelight we were looking at each other. "I will not forget you for a moment," he said.

I did not speak. I was exhausted. Agonizing moments. The only thing I wanted to say was, "Then let's go and leave this world that we both hate!"

As if he had read my thoughts, he said, "I am going. The longer I stay, the more difficult it will be to depart. But, before I go, may we dance together?"

The music outside had not stopped. In the candlelight, I stood up and, without thinking, rested my head on his shoulder. He threw his arms around my body. It felt like he was holding me in his arms. His lips kept kissing my hair. Being silent, we spun around like two wounded birds by the same arrow. I stopped for a second and said, "Sleep with me tonight!"

"What?"

"Sleep with me tonight! You just told me that I am your bride. I am yours. Only yours!"

He held me up in his arms like a crazy man, kissed me with passion and said, "Shush... I know our customs and traditions. The girl has to marry as a virgin. If not, the husband's people will return her to her parents as an action to disgrace for the whole family. I will never let this happen. In such a case this would destroy your family and your sick father. I cannot abuse them with this opportunity. Do you understand?"

"Yes, I do, but my life will be destroyed once and forever." I raised my voice when saying this, as if it was he the one to be blamed for everything.

"Okay," he said at last. "What do you want me to do? Tell me! Speak out!"

I was frozen for a few seconds. My eyes were like throwing out sparkles because of a thought that came to my mind.

"Let's go," I said. "Let's forget this world that brings only tears to both of us!"

"Okay," he said, "if you want that, come on. Let's do it! I would be the happiest man in the world. But I only think about you, because this would mean that there will be no turning back. You understand?"

"Turning back... I knew. Parents, sisters, the brother, and everything else I would never see anymore. This was the reality. The only thing that hit my head like a hammer was the thought of whether my father would be able to face and overcome this. I threw myself on a chair saying, "Well then, go! Go and don't turn your head back again! Let come what may! That's what is meant for me."

"No, no, don't....? he began to say.

"Just go, go immediately!" I raised my voice crying. "Leave me now, I am telling you!"

"Farewell!" he said in a broken voice. The door closed.

After he left I burst out crying. That room now seemed to me very dark as if it was my grave. My sister entered the room trying to calm me down. I stayed sleepless and crying all night. I kept praying to God that I would rather die before I went to the house of my future husband.

The dawn of that Sunday came with a gloomy cast. A boring rain made me feel like it was saying: "Do not worry, I am going to cry with you, too."

All my aunts by mother's and father's side, as well as our neighboring women, got together around me. My eyes were still swollen after all that crying.

"Make way, please! The hairdresser is coming to do her hair." She arrived, greeted and said, "Give me only twenty minutes!"

Everybody left the room and she started to fix my hair. "You seem tired," she said, "but still you are very beautiful." She continued to do the make-up, but never stopped talking. From outside a noise of a car was heard.

They came–came to take the bride. The children were shouting.

"They came on time," said the hairdresser.

In came my mother first, and then all the other women crowded around. Mother, tears in her eyes, kissed me on the forehead and whispered, "Happy life, my daughter!"

"Make way," a man's voice said. "We must bring the bride out to the new friends to see her." It was our oldest uncle. He grabbed me by the arm and said, "Follow me!"

Next came my father, holding me by the other arm. I wasn't sure whether he was holding me, or I was holding him. At the end of that alley there were a bunch of people formally dressed with ties on. Among them were two women beautifully dressed. They should be the bridegroom's sisters, for sure. My father met the new guests, and quickly turned to me, hugged and wished me, "Happy life, my daughter!"

I was turned into a live corpse whose tears, strangely enough, never stopped running down her cheeks. I felt the undertones of my sisters, cousins and other people around.

"That's enough now, enough! Let her go!" said the voice of the elder uncle, who was pulling me away. But my sisters did not want to release me. All of them, together with my mother, were crying silently. I felt like I was approaching death. When my uncle managed to separate me from my sisters' hands, I turned around and shouted, "Father, father!" With a bunch of fresh flowers in my hands, I stretched my arms out as if to tell him: I don't want to go, I don't!.... My calls 'father, father,' caused a silence in all that crowd of people looking curiously at what was happening. I saw regret in their eyes. Their eyes were expressing so much. Wedding is supposed to be the most beautiful day in one's life.

But not for many girls like me. The arranged marriage cuts off their dreams in the middle and sends them to an unknown world. My father knew this very well but would not accept being the first to break this wrong tradition for many girls living in small provinces of the country. Therefore he did not turn his head, but only raised his hands as if to say goodbye. Though I had turned my back to the car, two powerful hands pulled me away.

"Come on now, get in the car! You are ours now!" They actually pushed me forcibly to sit in the 5-seat jeep.

"Enough with these tears now," said one of the two women sitting by my side. She took a handkerchief and tried to wipe my tears. I pushed her hand away without speaking.

"Oh, she is even spiteful," she said.

"She is a bit waggish," said a man behind them, laughing.

That should be my future husband, I guessed. Now I was married. Married to a man I don't love, but others chose him for me. I felt something stirring my stomach, and put my hand on my mouth to let them know that I was throwing up. They stopped the car near a cold water spring. I threw up. This made me feel like my intestines were coming out of my belly as I had not eaten anything at all. I freshened up with some cold water and, like a child, returned to the car, looking at them with anger. They were smiling among themselves. We traveled for two hours and, at last, arrived at their house. All the wedding guests had come out to wait for the bride. Music, noises, unknown faces. I felt lost in a completely unknown world. From this very moment on, everything in my life was no longer under my control.

The next day and every day after, my mother-in-law would tell me what to do each and every day. I was responsible for the whole family: for cooking, washing clothes, and cleaning the house. My mother-in-law was really happy to command me. If she did not like something **I had** done, she would complain to her son, who now was my husband.

"She does not know anything at all. Her mother has not taught her. I have to watch her when she is doing anything." She threw out these darts all the time. On the other hand, you would hear him say, "She will learn, will learn."

When evening came, he used to punish me, sometimes by yelling at me, but now and then he would also beat me by hitting me hard on my face. It was not that simple to do everything on time for all ten people in that family. Much worse when I was pregnant. Almost six months had passed before I was, at last, allowed to see my parents and have some time with them.

On the way to my parents he ordered me, "Do not complain to them of many things; otherwise you will have consequences when back home." I did not speak. And he, as if reading my thoughts, said, "Hey, do you hear me, or not?"

"But what if I do not return at all?" I answered with the courage of a crazy person. He did not answer. Instead, he put his army boots on my foot and pressed it hard, very hard.

"Now you can answer me," he said scornfully, enjoying the fact that he could use force on me.

Maybe because of my anger, I did not feel much pain, though the skin of the upper part of my foot was cut deep and was bleeding on both sides.

"Wipe the blood," he told me with a commanding tone. You have even put on high-heeled sandals! Perhaps you still want to show off your beauty. But you must know that now you are my property. Do you hear me? You're mine!" He continued like an evil chatterbox all the way. When we approached my parents' village, he asked me,

"How many days you want to stay?"

"You know that I am your property," I said ironically. But it seemed that he liked this, and added, "I will decide later, after dinner."

My parents were very happy when they saw me.

"Poor me! God! What has happened to you? You look like a dead body! Completely pale! Do you eat or not?" My mother bombarded me with a number of questions. Father looked very surprised.

"Why do you look at me like that? You wanted me to marry him. This is what you wanted, the marriage! First, I am pregnant. Secondly, I must serve from early morning to late evening without any rest, otherwise punishment waits for me in the evening, being beaten by my husband."

My father, very upset, turned to my husband.

"What are these things I am hearing? We know the traditions, too, but to torture her like this, I don't accept. Daily bread she can eat here with us, too. Oh, no, this is unacceptable!" My father was speaking rather angrily.

"Do not worry, father, please," I interrupted. "Now everything is finished. I am expecting a baby. I am going to dedicate myself to the baby. Do you understand me?"

"No, no," continued father. "It is true that I married you, but no one has the right to raise his hand against you. You hear me?" Then he stood up from where he was sitting and turned to the bridegroom, who that moment had shrunk like a wet chicken.

"She is exaggerating," he said, moving a bit backward.

"Is that so, huh! Oh, what has happened to your foot? Why is it bleeding?"

I didn't speak. I did not want to add more pain to my parents' hearts. My mother brought some warm water in a washbasin and a small towel.

"Put your feet in here, my dear daughter!" She started to rub my feet in the washbasin with warm water.

"Our daughter will stay with us for some time," said father very decisively. "She needs to have some rest. If you think differently, you better never come back here!"

"But, well, let her stay some time," answered my husband. "Such are the customs. The bride has to do everything."

"But you," said father, "don't you help her at all? She is your wife, first of all. And will become mother of your children soon. What do you do? Or do you just stand by and watch?"

Father was shouting very angrily. My husband did not speak. He bent his head down as if he had understood or felt sorry. But I knew very well how much "sorrow" he was feeling: within himself he was burning with spite.

- "I'd better go," he muttered, "go before it is too late."

He stood up quickly and said, "Okay, then I will come back after two weeks. This would be enough for her to rest and relax. Huh, what do you say?" He was trying to smile to me.

"Just go! Get off for now and leave me in peace!" I slammed the door in his face as if to tell him, "Don't you understand that I don't want to see you anymore?"

The first week went by very quickly. Mother kept herself busy cooking and everybody was trying to lessen my spiritual pain. Each day I would go out to my father's fields to enjoy the endless beauty around. Perhaps the spiritual quietness and being among people that love and respect you, make you enjoy the beauties of nature. While I was thinking, I heard my sisters saying, "Come on, are you ready to go now?"

"No, you go! I will stay a little longer, okay?"

I heard them talking while they were walking away. I was left alone in the middle of that endless greenness. I lay down on the soft grass and opened my arms. My belly had grown a bit. My eyes were looking up into the blue sky, where I could see some clouds here and there. This very thing I used to do often when I was with Arbi. I closed my eyes and for a few moments recalled moments from the past. I stood up scared and spoke to myself: "What am I doing? Stop now! Now you are a married woman. It is shameful to think about someone else." My thoughts were interrupted by my father, who had just come up next to me.

"What are you doing here?"

"Nothing. I was just thinking."

"What do you say? Do you want to return or not?"

"To tell the truth, no, but now there is no other solution. This baby I have in my belly will be the only consolation. I will dedicate myself to my child."

"You have to excuse me, my daughter, you have to," said Father. "Now I understand everything. "But now you will have it easier. We'll be closer to you. Did you hear what is happening?"

"No." I looked up curiously.

"The youth now, your friends, all are looking for a new state power. And I am very sure that they will achieve it. I am very glad about that."

"Father, do you know what this means? This means freedom, democracy, new laws against violence on women. Oh, father! This really is an excellent news, indeed!"

Father embraced me and laughed happily when he saw me smile at last. We returned home. Lunch was ready for us. The smell of the warm pie had filled the house. I was eating and thinking.

At last we were reaching the goal. Oh, how much I wanted to be with them, with my friends to fight that wild communist beast in its last days. At least... I rubbed my belly with my hand…my child will be raised in democracy.

During whole second week with my parents I watched the news on TV every evening. Many young people were sacrificing their lives. Those in power were by all means trying to retain their power. But that was impossible now. It was too late for them. In the city streets you would see meetings almost every day organized against the ruling power. Young students and their professors were leading the people and you could hear them shout, "Freedom-democracy, freedom-democracy!"

Statues of the ruling leader were being pulled down. Houses and state buildings were set on fire. The people were very angry and fed up. All their lives people had been working under the leadership of a dictator. For 45 years on end there was only one leader. Only one leader who simply copied the style of other dictators in the East. But now he was dead and the fight to overthrow the government was being carried out against his successor. All those who were in power under him had to swear to him. The first toast in all weddings was not for the marrying couple, but always for the Communist Party and for the commandant Comrade Enver Hoxha. Though he was dead now, his bust had been in the main square of the capital city for what seemed like forever. Now that bust was being dragged along the streets by the Albanian democratic youth. This was the end of communism. Another world was being built in front of my eyes. I was very emotional. I was glad and scared at the same time before an unknown world. I looked up at walls of the dining room. Enver Hoxha's photo was still hanging there. And this, I believe, was in every household. I stood up, jumped on a chair and took it off the wall. Father did not react for the moment.

"You, the young, know it better," he said after a while.

"Thank you, Father. I don't expect you to understand everything that is happening, but it is important not to fight to protect the old system you were raised in. I know, Father, that it is very difficult for your age, but you are wiser than others."

He smiled and said, "I have smart girls."

After a while he added, "Eh, my daughter! I got used to you now, but tomorrow is Saturday, and your husband may come to take you home. As a matter of fact, I don't want you to go, but, on the other hand,..." He bent his head down looking at my belly. His eyes obviously were telling me: you are pregnant now.

"It's okay, Father. I trust that all will go well."

It happened as Father said. He came that Saturday to take me. I said goodbye to my family stirred by very strong emotions.

"Wait!" my father told him. "It's true that she decided to go with you. But you had better think and act very carefully! Okay?"

"Okay," he said hastily.

All the way back home I didn't say a word at all. Neither did he speak. He just kept smoking. The black smoke made his face gloomier. And there is their house, I was thinking. In that house I felt like somebody whom they had bought to serve them. The mother-in-law came out to wait for me and said, "Thank God you came! I am exhausted doing all housework! Now I have you."

"Stop that, mother! Because of you I almost lost my wife." That's how he spoke to his mother.

I turned my head without hiding my surprise. Perhaps my absence had made him think, or was he playing a fake role? She left angry. I had no other choice but to do all housework. He, my husband, did not stay home most of the time. He would go to work and after work stayed away entertaining himself with his friends. The only one who, I thought, felt sorry for me, was the father-in-law. One day I heard him tell his wife, "Hey, wife, enough with those orders because you are torturing the poor bride! Don't you see her belly grown so much? She will lose our baby. You hear me? I say, you have to stop it!"

I felt somehow better for this. I made three coffees and sat myself on the chair next to him.

"Here you are, Father!" I gave him the coffee with respect, but not to the mother-in-law. She grabbed the cup from the tray, saying, "You have made this coffee without foam! Go and make another one for me!"

"You take mine," her husband said angrily. "I want mine without foam."

She did not speak but looked at her husband with spite. I felt somehow pleased that I did not get up to make another coffee for her. I was drinking my coffee smiling from within. In the meantime I was feeling a light back pain. By the evening the pain became more severe.

"What is wrong with you?" asked my husband.

"I have a sharp pain in my belly and back."

"Take a spoon of olive oil and it will pass," he said, turning around comfortably in bed.

By the middle of the night the pain was unbearable.

"Please, send me to the hospital. I can't stand it anymore! And I don't know what is happening!"

He got up, whispering between his teeth, "She didn't leave me alone at least till morning!" The noise of the room door made others wake up.

"What has happened?" said the mother-in-law, who never missed anything going on in that house.

"She has pain. She is giving me a headache," he complained to his mother.

"Poor me! Maybe it is time for the baby delivery. But it's only seven months now! How can it be so?" she kept asking.

"I told you that she would lose the baby from the torture and hard work you give her," said the father-in-law.

"You better shut up! You always think the worst," she said.

"I will kill you if the bride loses the child!" said the father-in-law.

She did not speak. I stayed all that night in hospital in terrible pain. The doctor and nurses were very nice to me.

"You are at risk," said the doctor at last, "but as you are already in the seventh month we'll do our best for you to have a normal birth."

Next day at 4:00 p.m. after some indescribable pain, I heard the crying of a baby. Very exhausted, I tried to raise my head. They had wrapped the baby up in a white cotton blanket and were telling each other, "It's a boy, it's a boy!" That's what I heard and I don't know what happened next.

When I opened my eyes, I found myself in another room with beds on each side of me.

"The boy, please," I murmured with my dried lips. "I want to see him!"

The nurse looked up and said, "I will bring him. You may keep him for a few minutes, but we have to put him back into the incubator because the child is underweight."

I tried to raise my head and the nurse helped me get up in sitting position. Another nurse entered the room with a baby in her hands.

- "Are you ready?" she asked me. I stretched my hands out without answering. I couldn't stop staring at my baby. It was a very special feeling. I was touching his very tiny head, his little fingers folded into fists. Every part of him was so fragile that I was afraid I might give him pain each time I touched him. I rested my cheek on his lovely face. A more special feeling conquered all my being. I was feeling very happy. I had become a mother! I was only nineteen, but felt myself older than that. Now I would hold in my hands a human creature that I myself brought into existence! He will love me and I will love him for the rest of my life! This was a naturally made decision after one of the most momentous human experiences: childbirth!

"My son!" I said to myself. And, as if he heard me, he started to cry: "Wa, wa, wa!" It was a cry that was pinching my soul! I didn't know what to do with him. The nurse said, "Just breast-feed him!" She uncovered my breast, cleaned it with a soft cloth and warm water, and told me again, "Breast-feed him just like this." She put the baby at my breast, swollen with breast-milk, and baby's lips began to suck the milk at full pelt. Unbelievable! Just came to life and knew how to feed himself from mother's breast! While my baby was feeding himself, I kept fondling his little head. Stretched my hand and tried to open his tiny fist. He squeezed my finger. Great Lord! It was an indescribable feeling, new, strong, decisive! My son! My life! That was all. From now on I would never think anymore for myself. Everything would be about my son!

I stayed for some time in the hospital until my boy gained the necessary weight. When I returned home, it was rather difficult because not only had I to take care of the whole family, but now I had to take care of my own child. I would get up very early in the morning, irrespective of the sleepless nights. Even early in the day I felt completely exhausted. One day I took the courage to tell my husband, "It's enough. I can't take it anymore! My back is almost broken by the hard work. You must help me, otherwise I cannot survive."

At that time my child had reached six months. Instead of answering, he turned his back to me.

"Do you hear me or not?" I raised my voice. The answer was a hard fist to my face, which made my eyes blur for seconds.

"And you dare raise your voice?" he said. "Put your head down and work! Nothing will happen to you." And, on the way out, he added, "And listen here! I don't want to hear any more complaints from your mouth! Do you hear me?"

My eyes were swollen and in pain. I came back to myself only when I heard my son crying after being awakened by the noise. I quickly took him in my arms and tried to calm him down. My tears mixed with my child's. I wiped the tears and said, "My dearest soul! You have me here, why do you cry? Your mom is here! Here with you. With you, my son!" I continued to whisper while caressing him until he fell asleep. Looking at my delicate angel, I spoke, "You have your mother! But your mother has no one else. You grow, my son! Just grow! This is my life. I am turned into a servant. If I open my mouth in front of mother-in-law or my husband, a club will swipe my face. In my family I had never seen violence.

These were my thoughts when left alone. My husband thought that now, since I had a child, he could do anything he wanted with me. For me there was no turning back. Days were passing and my child was growing.

"You will never see violence, my son. You will grow with love and respect. But was this possible? I was wondering while I spoke all this silently. Oh, what an idiot I was! I was thinking too much about his future! I was going to discuss this sometime with my father. He was very mature and rational. Though in my case, with my marriage, he destroyed everything.

Life continued to become more and more difficult with every passing day. And each day had its unexpected events. Though I tried to do my utmost to avoid arguing with my mother-in-law or my husband, the following happened one day.

It was autumn. Autumn has always been one of my preferred seasons, though it becomes somehow melancholic before it's over. This may be due to the fact that at the beginning of autumn all kinds of fruits ripen, and flowers look still more beautiful after the hot summer air. But at the end of it, leaves, in all possible colors, start to fall on the ground. And so it happened that day, too.

After I had finished all the daily work, I went to my room for a short rest. Not more than ten minutes later I heard the voice of my husband:

"Hey, you! Where have you put your head?"

Rather scared, I got up and opened the door.

"What has happened?" I asked in half a voice.

"Some friends of mine are coming. In thirty minutes I want two broiled chicks, appetizers and brandy. I want to see the table full with everything. Did you hear me?"

When I looked at the watch on the wall, it showed 4:00 p.m.

"But I am very tired. Can you, please, make it with your friends another day?" I spoke humbly, hoping that he might change his mind.

"What?" he said. "Do you really want to disgrace me? Only thirty minutes you have! Poor you, if everything is not ready in time!" Then he left muttering profane things between his teeth.

I breathed deeply and silently and began preparing the table. In the meantime I had turned the oven on to broil the two chicks. "Take it easy," I said to myself. "Do whatever you can." Then I took some olives, fresh cheese, tomato salad, wine and brandy and put them hastily on the table. Looked at the clock again. Only ten minutes left. "Please, God, help me!" I said, running to the oven. The chicks were not yet done when four men and my husband entered the eating room. I heard them knocking their filled glasses and thought that everything was all right. When the chicks were ready, I put them on a large plate together with a big knife and a fork on the side. Holding it in my hands, I entered the eating room. I simply greeted them without raising my head, left the large plate on the table, and was making my way out.

"Wait!" he said, looking quite drunk. Grabbing me tightly by the waist he said, "You see, this is my wife! She does everything for me! Isn't it so?" he continued looking straight into my eyes.

I did not speak.

"Now you go and make a big pasty with cabbage for us. We are going to stay up the whole night! Don't you think so, my friends?" he said, very contented.

While moving away from him I spoke very carefully, "I am sorry, but I am very tired."

He was surprised, but did not speak. When they had finished everything on the table, they began to leave one after the other. I started to clean the table, asleep on my feet.

"Come on, we'll see you tomorrow!" I heard my husband's voice after he had seen off his friends. His steps seemed heavier and his walk showed him to be a drunken man.

"Hey, you! What was that? Did you want to try to disgrace me? Why did you defy me in front of my friends for what I told you to do when they came in?"

I raised my head and spoke, "I did not defy you. I am deadly tired. Look how my hands are shaking! Besides that, I am your wife and not your servant." I was speaking in a decisive voice without raising my head. He almost went mad.

"It seems that your mouth is back!" he said, seemingly surprised. "I'll kill you with my own hands."

"I don't care at all!" I answered. "I already feel dead anyway."

"Oh, yeah, okay! Now will I show you what death means!" And, speaking with his thickened tongue because of alcohol, he grabbed me by the arms and screamed, "Come on! Straight to the horses' stable! Hurry up!" Then, holding my arms, he dragged me away forcibly along the ground. Within five minutes I found myself in the middle of the horses. I felt so scared looking at the innocent faces of the animals.

I used to come often to fondle these animals in their stable. I used to feed them, clean them and speak to them. Yes, indeed. I used to speak to them. And, to my surprise, they did understand me, they did listen to me. It would often happen that when I was crying, and my tears fell on their necks while whispering to their ears, I could see tears in their eyes, too. Now, one of the horses came close to me, making the very familiar whinny for me. He seemed to ask me, "Why don't you fondle me? What is happening?" I reached my hand out and fondled his foamy lips.

"It's okay, it's okay!" I said to him. That horse was very dear to me. He was the most beautiful and wisest of all. The muscles in his body rippled. To me it seemed as if a famous sculptor had made a gigantic sculpture. Such a quiet and beautiful creature was that horse to me. I had already forgotten for a moment why I was there. But this did not last long. The husband's voice, like a screeching crow, yelled again, "Give me the whip!"

I was frightened and shaking all over unaware of what was going to happen to me. Not thinking, he jumped on the back of the same horse I was fondling a moment earlier.

"I am going to show you what it means to be a man! I am the man, and you have to obey! If not, then there isn't any other way for you!" While screaming like that, he kept whipping the poor horse. The horse kept shying and neighing loudly.

"Please, do not hit the poor animal!"

He stood close in front of my face.

"I will kill you and the horse!" he yelled wildly again.

"Come on! Heave-ho!" he was calling, screaming and whipping the poor animal. "Move forward, you dirty animal!" As he struck the horse wildly and brutally, I was feeling as if each lash on the horse's body was hitting me, too. Tears were running down from the big eyes of the horse. And it seemed to me that his tears and mine had the same rhythm.

"Don't, please!" I called out loudly, stretching my hands toward the horse. But he ignored my cry and continued, "Come on! Go ahead! I don't feed you for no reason, you dirty animal! Walk ahead! Walk!" And the whip kept flying up and hissing in the air, leaving swollen lines on the horse's back.

Oh! How much hatred I felt at that moment! I really pitied the poor horse. He, my husband, was using the horse to kill me! But the horse seemed as if he understood his goal and stood still, not moving an inch. And me, already frozen like a statue, was only two feet away from the horse.

When my husband felt tired after all his hard efforts, he got down from the horse and said, "No one wants to listen to me anymore in this house, whether I speak in a nice way or in a brutal way!" And, because of his crazy spite, he pushed me forcibly and added, "If you will not listen to what I order you to do, the whip will be waiting for you!" Then he left in a fury.

I slowly tried to get up from a pile of manure where I was thrown. My whole body was trembling. I turned my eyes to the poor animal.

"Trojan, come over here, please!" I had named him Trojan since he was a little animal. Now he was noisily snorting and running from one side of the stable to the other. I was afraid to approach him. He seemed confused. I wanted to smooth his wounds, his neck and his tearful eyes.

After a few minutes Trojan came close to me and started to make the usual noise. He was blowing up in rage and snorting yet with anger.

I brought my head closer to his and he did not go away. Then, resting my head on his, I started to speak.

"I am sorry for you--sorry! You do not deserve to be beaten like this. Why? You are so loving, wise and innocent. While speaking like that, I felt Trojan's tears join mine. I raised my head to see his big eyes. His head did not move at all. He kept it down and his eyes were, surprisingly, deeply sad. Tears kept running from his eyes again. I had never seen an animal cry like a human being. Or perhaps I had not noticed it before. I hugged the poor animal as if it were a human being.

"I promise you," I said, "that I will never let him touch you again. You go now! Wherever you want! At least you'll be free. While speaking to him, I untied the rope and told him again: "Just go now! Go!"

Trojan cantered around me a few times as if trying to decide what to do. After that he neighed with a screeching voice. His front legs sliced the air. The stable door was open.

"Come on, go now!" I said. He went out reluctantly. After a few moments the noise of his steps faded away.

"You are free, free," I whispered to myself. My heart was gushing with joy because, at last, my Trojan obeyed me. Still this did not last very long. When I was getting ready to leave that stable, I heard the steps of Trojan coming back again.

"Oh, no, no! You go, just go!" I was speaking to him a bit harshly. Trojan came next to me and did not move an inch. He blew up a few times with anger just as if to say: I cannot let you alone. I can't. Then I hugged him silently. I brought him back into the stable, and, caressing him again, I said, "Lie down and rest!" Trojan obeyed immediately. Unbelievable! Trojan was understanding everything I told him. I sat next to him, and I don't really know how long I stayed like that. I had fallen asleep right there in that stable resting myself on the warm neck of Trojan. And it was only when one of my sisters-in-law came to take me, that I woke up. I kissed Trojan slightly just not to wake him up. After that I went away in slow steps into the darkness. Cursed be this darkness! This life! These people who create this cursed darkness! No, no. Better say this horror!

I had turbulent thoughts in my head: darkness, shackles, people, sun, rain, a rainbow. The head of Trojan appeared among the images, but this time just a unicorn next to the rainbow. And pitch darkness again! Endless darkness! I was moving, plunging ever deeper into that darkness that was killing me. I had fallen to the ground completely powerless. This I understood only when I heard my sister-in-law calling me, "Get up! Let's go inside! Come on! Clean yourself and go to bed! You need to relax and calm down. Cursed be my brother!" She whispered to herself. "Cursed be the customs of this country and everything else that tortures us women." I obeyed her and held fast to her arms.

After having a shower, I went to kiss my son, the only love in that house. He was sleeping like an angel. When he felt my kiss, he turned to me and hugged me. I slept next to him shedding fresh new tears in silence.

I want freedom! Only my freedom together with you, my son! That night was long, endless, and pitch-dark. And I, plunged into that darkness, was searching to see, even a tiny window full of light. I was in search of freedom!

Three years had already passed since the birth of my son. Sufferings and endless vicissitudes only an idiot like me could stand up to and endure. All the time I kept thinking, I have a son. I must raise him in the best way possible. I was watching how he was growing every day, and I had already changed myself into a rag doll. When I saw myself in the mirror, I just exclaimed: 'Gosh! What have I become?' I had simply turned into a housewife, or better said, a slave. Except for raising my boy, everything else I did without any zest or more accurately, I was forced to do the rest. I never had time enough to think about myself and other things.

One day I was somehow quieter. My husband had gone somewhere on business for some days. His parents were visiting mother-in-law's relatives. This gave me some time to rest a little and take care of myself. When I was looking myself in the mirror, I could see here and there the wounds on my body because of the violence my husband had used on me. Many blue lines looked like a map over my naked body.

Is this my life? I asked myself. Real torture! According to the tradition, he was allowed to do whatever he wanted to me. Whenever he returned home, if he heard any complaints, I would be judged by the family trial, like why haven't you done this well? Or, why are you absent-minded? And each question was followed by a violent fist to my face.

Thinking back on all the events that had taken place against me, all of a sudden a new idea crossed my mind: What if I took my son and returned home to my parents? To go back to my people that love and respect me? To return to my dreams where they had been cut off in the middle?

That day only the little brother-in-law was at home with me. He was about fourteen. Very quickly I put on a dress, made my hair pigtail, differently from other days, and covered my face and hair with a white scarf. Then I put some clothes for my son into a suitcase that was in the wardrobe. On my way out, my little brother-in-law asked, "Where are you going?

"I am going to the hospital as my son is not feeling well." He did not intervene anymore, but I had the impression that he understood what was happening.

I did not turn my head back. My heart was beating fast. The way to the bus-station was some fifteen minutes walk. Perhaps I made that distance in five minutes.

Tired and breathing heavily, I put my son on the ground and told him, "You sit on that suitcase, okay?"

"Where are we going?"

I did not answer, but smiled instead. Actually I was very scared. What if a member of the family returned? What if he himself came back? Then, who knew what would happen to me? Looking left and right like a prisoner who had escaped the jail, I saw the bus taking the turn and it stopped three steps away from me. Quickly I grabbed the suitcase and my son, entered the bus, and kept looking outside through the window.

I hope I escaped! I embraced my son and spoke to him, "We are going to my mother, okay?"

"Oh, to the mother, to the mother?" he said that happily simply because he was going somewhere. When the bus had passed the area of my husband's house and entered the village area where my parents lived, I felt I could breathe deep and freely. Still I was thinking that the bus would not bring me to my house. It would stop somewhere near my village. Then I had to find a taxi. While thinking all these thoughts and playing with my son on the bus, in front of me, I saw an old mother and a boy about my age sitting next to her. Shameless and courageously, he asked, "Where are you going, lady?"

Though still afraid to answer, in a shivering voice, I said, "To my mother."

"For how long you have not seen her?" he asked me.

"I don't know," I answered hesitantly.

"How long will you stay there?" he said.

I looked up and very proudly said, "Forever."

"What? Aah! I understand," he continued .

But I did not want to listen to him anymore. Instead I turned my head to the window looking at the free world, and kept kissing my son repeatedly on the head, cheeks, and neck. At last I'd managed. The bus stopped. I carefully stepped off the bus.

"Wait for me to help you!" he said.

Without talking at all, I gave him the suitcase with my son's clothes. He found a bench for us to sit comfortably.

"You'd better rest a bit, then ask for a taxi!"

I fed my son and gave him some fresh water from a spring nearby. While we waited for the taxi, he fell asleep. I put him carefully on the bench, and then put some clothes under his head. In that quiet sleep in the fresh air he looked like an angel. I went to the spring and freshened myself up. When I raised my head up to avoid wetting my hair, the boy accompanying me, who had not left yet, noticed a large bruise on my neck.

"He seems to have been an animal!" he said. "Now I understand why you are going away. What is your name?" He asked me that question with respect.

"It doesn't matter," I said quickly, feeling a bit scared.

"Do not be afraid. I only want to help you."

"Thank you! I will manage somehow to get home."

"That's okay then. I live here nearby. You may come and rest for a while. I have my mother and sister at home."

"No way," I quickly cut it short.

"Then I will be waiting here till the taxi comes. Only after that can I go home and feel comfortable," he said decisively.

I did not refuse. My son was still sleeping quietly. Adding to my anxiety, no vehicles were passing by.

"What is your name?" he asked for a second time.

"Ema," I said somehow ashamed.

"Very beautiful," he said. "My name is Robert. Soon I will go to Germany. Just waiting for the visa to be ready."

I did not speak.

"Listen! You speak to your parents. If you want, I can help you. Just to get away from this place!"

I looked at him coldly. He understood and said, "I am not exploiting this opportunity at all! I know that I'm talkative, but I simply am trying to help you."

"Indeed?" I asked skeptically.

"Yes, yes," he said.

"Then can you, please, go to my neighborhood number eight and inform my cousin to come and pick me up. His name is Arthur."

"Turi? Hey, but he is my friend!" he said, smiling.

"Come on, let me take you there!"

It was somewhere near, but to me it seemed like a long walk. Maybe it was because of the hot day or I was tired holding my son in my arms. And I don't know why I obeyed a stranger and was following him.

"I live here," he said after a while. He ran inside and came out quickly together with his sister.

"We'll accompany her to Arthur's," he was telling her sister. She has got some problems."

Off we went. He led us. Me and his sister followed behind. We had passed only five houses when he stopped in front of a big iron door.

"Do you recognize their home?"

"No," I said, "it's been a long time since I've visited." He knocked on the door and shouted, "Hey, Turi! Open the door—quickly!"

From inside I heard the very well known voice of my aunt, "Turi is not here."

"That's okay. You're Turi's mother? Please open the door!"

The aunt came closer and looked through a hole on the iron door.

"Wow! Wow! What's wrong with you? Oh, my dear niece! What has happened?"

She took the boy from my hands and said, "Come on in, what are you waiting for?"

They both, brother and sister, stopped at the front door and said, "We'd better go! Now you are in safe hands," he said.

"Goodbye then!" His sister squeezed my hand as a sign of respect. The boy, Robert, approached me and said, "Remember, if you want to go to Germany, you talk to Turi, okay?" He was looking straight into my eyes. How courageous! His way of looking at me made me speak quickly without thinking.

"I wish you a safe trip! Good luck, wherever you go!" I smiled and I don't know why I felt that free with him. I hugged him as if hugging Turi, my cousin.

"I forgot to tell you something," he whispered in a low voice, "You really are a very charming woman, very beautiful! I will be waiting to hear from you through Turi."

I turned away quickly to make him understand that he had to leave. He raised his hand, walking backward. "Goodbye, again!" And walking that way, I heard him stumble and fall. We both laughed and I entered the house thinking: there are a lot of good people, too, in this world.

In the meantime my aunt had put my son to sleep on a little bed She came out saying, "Come on, dear. Tell me what has happened!"

"I am exhausted, aunt," I said while taking off my dress, wet from sweating.

"Oh, dear me! What has he done to you?" She left with tears in her eyes and returned soon with a big towel and some clean clothes.

"Go and have a shower."

I did not speak. I took the clothes and had a long shower. Afterward I dressed, covered my hair with the towel, and lay down next to my son. I had no idea how long I slept. But when I got up, I heard my aunt speak,

"How is it possible to torture a girl that age? And why?"

From the other room I heard the voice of my uncle, her brother, who seemed to have come for a visit.

- Unacceptable!

I got up and joined them.

"Where is my son," I asked, after I hugged my uncle.

"I fed him and he is playing now. Don't worry about him!"

"Did Turi come? I must go home."

"We sent Robert to get him, otherwise he would return late."

Turi entered, hugged me gently and said, "Let's go to my room."

Turi and me were the same age. I spoke quite long with him. He listened quietly and said, "I only have one question for you, "Have you thought enough about this matter? You know well that he is going to fight for it."

"Yes," I said, breathing deeply. "I am scared and I don't hide it. But something had to be done. It was impossible to live like that."

"You are right. One more question. Have you done something that causes him to treat you this way? I mean," he spoke blushed in his face, "have you gone out with another man?"

"Never! It's my honor and pride. First, I do it for myself, not for him," I said angrily.

"I know. You have to excuse me, but before we make the first step toward your freedom, we must make sure not to end in a blind alley."

"For this I assure you with my life."

I answered him with love.

Now I was understanding that, by leaving my husband, a war had already been declared unintentionally. He, my husband, would not give up easily. First he would feel ashamed in the eyes of the village because his wife had left him. Secondly, he knew that he was nobody without me. Maybe now he was going to feel for real what I had been doing in that house. Not only he, but all his family. But I didn't care at all about it.

So it happened indeed. When only a few days had passed since I returned to my family together with Turi, and the blue bruises on my body were not healed yet, he and his elder brother came. His elder brother tried to show himself more respectful. But actually he never cared for anybody. Only when his family's interests were at stake, like in this actual case, he would involve himself.

My father and Turi received them with respect, but very vigilant, too.

His elder brother spoke first, "I understand that your daughter has been treated unjustly, but from now on I am going to take the matter into my own hands. He and your daughter will buy a house in town. He has now understood what he has lost and apologizes for that. Isn't it so?" he asked his brother.

"Yes," he said. "So were our traditions and I didn't know how to act, but now...."

- "Stop!" spoke my father furiously. "To me you are a bastard, indeed. Nevertheless the decision will be made by my daughter. It was enough that I destroyed her life with my former decisions. Times are changing now. But it seems that time never changes for people like you. Now stand up and get out of here once and for all."

They did not move from their seats. Then Turi stood up. This meant ... *Out of here, otherwise....* After this, being a difficult situation, they stood up.

"We are leaving, but this will not end here. If she will not come with us, then we are going to keep the son."

"What?" said my father very angrily. "Get out of here! Out, bastards!"

While the elder brother went out, my husband returned and said, "We'll return again. I want to speak with my wife."

When they had disappeared beyond the outer door, my mother made coffee for all of us.

"Make it strong, without sugar!" said my father, blushed completely with anger.

"Calm down!" said Turi. "I am going to stay here for some days until this matter is settled." So, father was calmed somehow. They kept discussing. I heard Turi say, "It is democracy now. They cannot use force anymore to take Ema or the son."

"I know, I know it well," answered Father, but laws are not yet in power or functioning. I don't see it that simply."

Only five hours had passed when, at about 5:00 p.m. he, my

husband, appeared again.

"What do you want?" said my mother.

"I want to speak with the host of the house."

Father, who heard him, said, "Come inside. Sit! Say what you have to say!"

He started to cry like a child. "I know that I have made mistakes. I want you to forgive me. Give me another chance! Please!"

Father did not speak.

- "Please!" he continued. "I bought a new house in the city near you. I don't live with them anymore. They destroyed me. From now on I will take care of my wife and the child."

Saying this, he blamed his family.

"I heard you," said father, "but still I will not be the one to decide. This time it will be my daughter who will make the decision for herself."

"But, may I speak with her?"

"Yes," said father. "Ema, Ema, come here, my daughter!"

I came out of the room very proudly, though within me still there was some fear. I sat next to my father. My father spoke and explained to me the conditions and about the house he had bought somewhere near my parents.

"No, I can't," I said quickly. "I cannot forget how much I have suffered in that family."

"I know, I know. But from now on I will change. I promise."

"No," I said quietly, and went out.

Then, angrily, he said, "I will take the son."

At that moment, I don't know from which room it came, but I heard the voice of my son,

"Mammy, Mammy!" He came to the living-room and threw himself into my arms. Then he saw his father.

"Daddy, Daddy!" He kept the son in his arms for some moments and then took an airplane doll out of his pocket and gave it to him.

"This is for you!"

Our son walked back and forth in the room playing with the airplane.

"My father brought it to me! This is my airplane!"

All were looking at him without saying anything. It had created a very touching situation that made us feel and look upon with regret.

"We'll give you an answer tomorrow," said father.

"Okay," he said, looking around with some ray of hope.

"Your father is right. You have to think about it first. Do you see your son? Last of all, you are married now. All make mistakes." My mother was saying all these words while staring at the firewood in the stove.

"Mammy, they were not mistakes!" I shouted with a feeling of pain.

Perhaps my parents were hesitating because they felt ashamed that their daughter had left her husband. This sounded unprecedented.

"Then you have to think about the son. He has to be raised with parents. Isn't it so?"

I didn't speak. I went into the room and flung myself down on the bed. I didn't know what to do. Next day he came back again and started from the beginning.

"The house is in the center of the city. I have also bought the furniture and everything is ready. Please!" he continued. "Don't worry! If I treat you wrong again, you may leave whenever you want. You hear me?"

My parents were not speaking. Neither did Turi. Being in that very unpleasant situation I made the biggest mistake in my life. I grabbed my son by the hand and said, "Let's go!" My son held his father by the other hand and after that I did not turn my head behind. I just left. I left without knowing where I was going.

Everything took its flow quickly after this. The new house, the city and all around us drew me into the daily impetus of something new. Life around me was changing every day. Now I was already a housewife in my own house. The son went to kindergarten every day. Now I had time to not only take care of the house, but of myself, too. Opposite my apartment, I had a very good neighbor. She was a gynecologist physician. Each afternoon, after she returned home from the job, we used to drink coffee together. She taught me many things. She was surprisingly energetic. One day I asked her, "How did you manage to become a physician?"

"I had to sacrifice my family for that," she said.

"What about now?"

"Now we have rejoined," she said and smiled.

"Have you ever been in love?"

"Yes, I have loved my profession as a physician."

I did not speak.

"What about you?" she asked me after a moment.

First I looked around not to be seen by anybody.

"Yes," I said, somehow ashamed.

"Is it he whom you have today?"

"No, I could not marry him. It's a long story…" I waved my hand as if to say better forget about it now.

"Do you still have feelings for him?"

I looked up scared.

"I don't know what to say. I am married. Still, I continue to think about him sometimes. I have not forgotten him, though I try to do so."

"But, what has happened to him?" she continued.

"How can I know? He must have married some other beauty, for sure." I said this, bending my head down. She became almost ready to say something else, but I interrupted her by saying,

"That's enough! I feel like it's not worth talking about it anymore."

"Okay, okay!" she said and took some big apples from the fridge.

"I still can't stop thinking about it: how is it possible that you don't want to talk about your love?" She said this after a few moments, while putting a peeled apple on my little plate.

"But that's not so simple actually. The fact is I am married and I have a son, too. I am sacrificing everything for his sake. I want him to grow a happy person and have everything." While speaking I kept moving my hand up and down as a sign of nervousness. I didn't know why this discussion was disturbing me.

"And how do you get along with your present husband?" she asked me, not looking in my eyes.

"What shall I say? He seems to have changed a bit. I don't suffer as I did before in the village, where I served his whole family. Now it's not that I have any feelings for him. I just do everything mechanically. Anything he says is a law in the family. That is how it is."

"But now things are changing," she interrupted before I finished. "Women are a powerful part of democracy. Why don't you become part of it? If you don't like something, just say no. Express your opinion freely."

She was speaking and I was thinking. How intelligent this woman is! She knows many things!

"I will be here for you for any problem you may have," she continued.

"Thank you," I said, smiled and was ready to go. I was just saying goodbye to her, when I heard a knock on the door.

"I am sure that's my husband," she said and hurried to open the door.

"Oh, it's you! Come inside."

"No, no. I wanted ...." said the very familiar voice of my husband.

"Hold on, she is coming." The door was left half open and she whispered into my ear, "You take care of yourself!"

"Good-bye," I said quietly.

As soon as I entered my house, I caught the scent of the alcohol he had drunk.

"What are you doing? Are you crazy? What do you want with that neighbor?"

"I was having a coffee." I spoke coldly and turned my back to him. The doctor's words "Take care of yourself" were still buzzing in my head.

"You don't turn your back on me!" he shouted. "I don't want you to step out of this house! Do you get me, or not?"

He was shouting, shaking his hand close to my face.

Angrily I told him, "I am not afraid of you!"

Very surprised, he put his hands around my throat and was yelling at me, "I'll kill you if you do things your way!" Then he threw me on the bed. Tearing off my clothes, he continued shouting, "Perhaps that bitch is teaching you! She poses like an intelligent woman! But you are my wife. My wife! Otherwise you are gone! And not only you, but your son, too! Did you understand it?"

He grabbed my jaw in a firm grip and I bit him with my teeth forcefully on his hand and screamed loudly, "You are an animal and so will you remain forever!"

A powerful blow to my face blurred my eyes. I don't know, but when I opened my eyes, I saw my face wet, with blood running from my nose. I stood up. I did not feel any pain at all. A cold feeling for him had only grown with the years. And now that feeling was much more powerful and much more frigid. He had left the room and, as if nothing had happened, was eating dinner very calmly.

After a short moment he said, "Come and sit near me!"

I did not speak. I felt the pain in my lips when I tried to open my mouth.

"You have to excuse me," he continued. "Sometimes I get angry and don't know what to do. But you know how crazy I am about you. I will not hit you anymore."

"You will never change!" I said very coldly. I went to the room and threw myself next to my boy, who was sleeping. I started to fondle his soft hair, but my tears woke him up, and he saw the blood.

"What is it Mammy? Why do you cry?"

"Nothing, my son. Nothing. Sleep now, your Mammy is here with you!"

He kissed my hand, put it on his chest and held it tight to his body. At that time he was only four. Nights like this would be repeated often. He would return home drunken and I had to try to calm my son down, for he was often scared by his father. One morning I was very exhausted, felt dizzy and was ready to throw up. After sending my son to the kindergarten I went to talk to the doctor, who was my neighbor. Her office was somewhere nearby.

After a few questions, she said quietly, "I was afraid that it would happen."

"Happen what?" I asked her quickly.

"You are pregnant. Nevertheless, congratulations!" She squeezed my right hand soberly.

I did not speak, but after this I felt that everything was over for me. Two children with the man I did not love at all! How stupid I was! Worst of all he was my husband. Could having a sibling positively influence the boy?

After some days I gave him the news.

"I am pregnant," I said very nervously while folding some washed clothes.

"That's better yet. With two children you will lose your elegance, and I will, at last, feel better." He was boasting and flashing his cunning smile, as well.

"After some months I will leave for Greece to work. You will stay with your parents. When you deliver the baby, my elder brother and his wife will help you. Now he is the chief of the police financial department, and has great influence in the community."

I didn't say anything. The idea that he would be away from me made me feel good.

"You seem not to be concerned that I will leave!" he said with a humorless grin.

"Maybe you will become wiser and make up your mind there, wherever you go." I continued stirring the tomato sauce.

He laughed and came near me.

"I will miss oregano's smell in fresh sauce."

"That's okay because you will pollute it with the perfume smell of the street girls."

"How do you know that I deal with street girls?" He looked scared. "I am not that kind of a person."

"I did not say that you deal with them. It simply was a joke," I said. Since I'd known him he not only drank, but most of the time was out having fun elsewhere.

"Last of all, I am a man," he said. "And men can do anything whenever they want to do it."

His words reminded me again of the words my mother often said: When a girl is born even the leaves of trees weep." Now I understood what she meant. A female must submit herself to the male all through her life. I rubbed my belly with my hand. Perhaps it may be a girl, or another boy? One thing I knew well. I would teach my child to have respect for others, be it a man or a woman. Perhaps the same thing was happening with the whole new generation. Many young adults had already broken the old rules long ago.

While lost in thought, I heard my son tell me, "It's mother, mother! Mother is coming!" He had seen my parents from the balcony. Feeling glad, I went to see them from the balcony, too. My uncle was with them, as well. A little surprised, I opened the door while they were coming up to the 4th floor.

"You are very welcome!"

My uncle entered first. We hugged each other. My parents didn't speak for a while. My husband, at times used to ask my uncle how he was doing with his health.

"Nothing happens to us. You, the young, have to be careful," said the uncle very seriously.

These words sounded bitter to my husband, and somehow frightened, he turned to me and said, "Have you complained to them, or what?"

"No, but perhaps today I will do so."

- He made the sign: *I'll cut your head off!*

Fearlessly I stuck out my tongue as a sign of ridicule. He turned his back trying to pretend calmness.

"We have heard some words about you," started my uncle. "They say that you have already started to drink and make scandals out there in the streets."

"Indeed! That's interesting! What else is left unsaid by you?" I asked him.

"No, no. These are all rumors," said my husband again. "You shut up!" he shouted at me, forgetting that my people were there.

"That's okay," said the uncle. "But be careful! This would be the end of you."

He stood up looking very furious:

"You better calm down!" my uncle said. "Today we have come simply to have a coffee. Next time it will be you who tells us what bad thing has happened to you." My uncle was drinking his coffee quietly. They did not stay long.

"Huh, she!" he was shouting and walking back and forth. "What does this mean? I can't stand it at all! I can't accept anybody giving me orders.

"Oh, indeed?" I said. "But just put yourself for a moment in my position! You give me orders all the time! Can you see now how I may feel about you?"

"You are a woman," he continued.

"Today the woman has the right to speak and the right to become anything in life."

"Enough, enough! You seem to me like a politician when you speak like that. Stop! I can't stand for you to speak like a man! Women are only housewives and give birth to children. And so will it continue to be in the future! Only like this!" He was now shouting..

Many more days passed like that. He went back and forth very nervous and all the time drunken. At last, one day I saw him go out with a back-bag.

"I am going. Going to Greece. Whenever I am able, I will send you something to feed yourself and the child."

I had no feelings at all for the fact that he was leaving. On the contrary, I was thinking: 'God, let him go! Away with him!'

Maybe I should apologize to God, I was telling myself. But for some months I felt much better having him away from me. The day of delivering my second child was coming soon. He had told me that his people would take care of me and my son the day of delivery. But I was thinking that it would be better to ask my mother to come for some days, instead. And so I did. My mother was happy to have the opportunity to take care of me.

"I have heard a lot about hospitals these days," said my mother very concerned.

"What?" I asked her.

"Well... you see, there is a turmoil actually. The doctors don't help at all if you don't pay them. That's what I have heard from..."

"That's enough, mother! What are you saying?"

I don't know why I didn't want to hear her talk like that. I was scared for the very fact that I didn't have any money at all. At this moment I remembered his last words: my brother will help you. But his brother had never appeared at all. Perhaps he knows the day of birth. Perhaps his brother had advised him when and what to do. Two days before delivery his brother came to send me to the hospital.

"May God save you, my daughter! I will take care of the boy."

And so I left, hugging mother and my son. At the last moment I told the son, "Mammy will bring you a beautiful baby from the hospital." He kissed me on the belly.

"Okay Mammy! Please bring me chocolates and some toys, too."

"Sure, you are Mammy's soul."

In the meantime I was cudgeling my brain about what was going to happen to me. I had not a penny in my pocket. Was it true that corruption had spread all over? Was it true that doctors would not help if you didn't pay them cash? Would they simply let you die? Still I tried to calm myself down. No, this could not be true. How could it be like that? Actually I was left alone at my brother-in-law's house. The sister-in-law had gone out with her husband. Only their son, Jorgo, was with me.

"Jorgo, would you like something to eat?"

"Yes," he said with that characteristic smile of a child. When laughing, two dimples formed on his cheeks. He was one year older than my son. I fed him and played for a while with him. When he seemed tired, I picked him up in my arms and put him in bed. When I got up from the chair I felt a sharp pain at the bottom of my belly. I knew well what was about to happen. Immediately I prepared all the clothes for delivery, like white sheets, some cotton napkins and pajamas. When I had prepared everything, my brother-in-law and his wife came in.

"What is going on?" they asked me.

"Today is the time," I said, straining my muscles because of the sharp pain.

"Okay," said the brother-in-law to his wife. "You go with her, and I will stay with Jorgo."

We walked all the way to hospital. It was only about twenty minutes. At moments I had terrible pain, at others it was easier.

"Your husband should be with you now," said my sister-in-law, somehow nervous. "Why should I run around with you?"

She continued to say such things, but, due to my unbearable pain, I did not hear anything. I could only see that she was unhappy with this situation.

"You may go back if you want to," I murmured, in great pain.

"Wow!" she exclaimed, not wanting anyone she knew to see her walk away. From that moment she didn't speak until we entered the hospital. As soon as we were in, she said abruptly, "Now I am going back home."

I did not say a word and did not turn my head either. I was left alone. I had nobody to stay with me. The nurses put me in a waiting room where many other women were sitting. I had to wait for over two hours in that room, where now and then screams were heard by women in pain. At that time in my country it was out of question to think about pain killers. All births were carried out naturally. My pain was ever increasing and I could not bear it anymore. I had to grab a passing nurse by her arm, and ask, "Please, I can't stand it anymore! Pains are almost non-stop."

She looked at me, and, seeing my tears running down my face, because of the terrible pain," she asked me, "Who is here with you?"

I hung my head and said, "I have nobody now, but my brother-in-law will come, and I have his telephone number here." Her question meant "Who is going to pay me?" I understood it very well. Therefore I had put some ten thousand Leks under my shirt. I spoke crying. "But when my brother-in-law comes he will maybe pay more...... "Aah! Oh!" I shouted again. She did not wait anymore; she grabbed the money from my hand and told me, "Lie down! I will examine you!" She put her hands on my belly to see the position of the baby.

"Put your legs up here," she said, and, after putting a pair of gloves on her hands, she examined me silently.

"You are ready now. Let's go to the delivery room." I could hardly follow her.

"You just sit over there!"

After a few minutes a doctor and a nurse came in. The one I paid did not appear anymore.

"Push!" said the doctor. "I do not have much time to be with you."

"Push! Push!" She put her hands over my belly and was shouting: "Come on! Bring it out! What are you waiting for? Push more!"

It was an indescribable pain shooting through my body. I couldn't stop groaning. Sweat and tears mixed together. My hair became wet. I could not comfort myself, and just when I was breathing deeper the doctor was shouting again, "Go ahead! Push hard!"

I strained to the maximum and pushed my baby out. After this I felt as if my head had been cut off and fell on the pillow. But, as if in the sleep, I heard my baby's voice

"Wa - wa..." I closed my eyes feeling happy that I had achieved my goal. I don't know how many minutes I stayed like that. When I opened my eyes, I felt quite cold. I saw someone passing by.

"Please, what was the baby? Boy or girl?"

"Wait for the doctor to come!" said the nurse and bent her head down. I didn't like at all the way she did that.

"What has happened?" I tried to get up, but it was impossible.

The doctor appeared at the door. It was the doctor who assisted in my delivery.

"Yes," I asked. "What was it? Please bring the baby here!"

Her face looked very cold.

"What shall I show you?" she said. "You gave birth to a dead child. We could not save the child. We did not have enough oxygen."

"What? There is no oxygen?! Oh, no!" For a while I had forgotten that the country I was living in was poor. And during the transition period from communism to democracy many doctors were corrupted. If you did not pay them a hefty amount of cash money in hand, they wouldn't care what happened to the patient. Only if they were satisfied with the money you paid, then the patient would receive the proper attention. I want to stress here that not all doctors were like this. There were a lot of them who had remained human and continued to work with real devotion. However, to my bad luck, I did not have a large amount of money in hand for the doctor who assisted at my delivery.

And now I was hearing: There is no oxygen... What a horror! A child dies for lack of oxygen! From what I was hearing everything around me seemed very hopeless. Each word that came out of doctor's mouth was being interpreted quite differently in my mind. The fact that I lost my child made me look at the whole team working around me with a frozen feeling in my soul. I put my hands on my head and screamed, "No, no, no! It is impossible! No, I want my baby! No, I can't believe this! I cannot..."

I tried to pull myself together, and, with all my strength got up in a sitting position in bed. The doctor who told me about what had happened was still there.

"You are neither the first nor the last," she continued. "Pull yourself together! Life continues!"

After these words, my hatred for that doctor became extreme. I turned around toward her and, screaming like a wolf bitch, struck her with all my strength and told her to get out of my sight as I couldn't listen to her anymore. She moved a few steps back, ordered others to give me tranquilizers because I was crazy, and disappeared. Then everybody left the room. I was alone in the delivery room howling to the sky again: "My baby! I want my child! Please, bring him in!"

I felt my eyes fill with tears. The whole room looked pitch black to me. I felt something warm wetting my back side. I checked with my hand to see what it was.

"Blood! Much blood!" I heard them saying as if in a dream. "A woman is dying! A woman is dying. Hurry up!"

Hearing this, I felt sorry for that woman who was dying!

Feeling myself like in a heavy sleep I couldn't open my eyes. Nevertheless I could whisper : "How sad that a woman is dying. The woman is .... dy ...ing..... where ... is my... baby....?... I ...want...the ... baby...."

I didn't know how long I had been sleeping. When I opened my eyes all parts of my body were in pain. I felt tubes in my mouth, nose and arms. I saw my mother sleeping on a chair next to me. Her hand held mine tightly.

Why! When did she come here? "Mommy," I whispered, "Mommy!" I tried to speak in a full voice, and tried to move her hand away.

Surprised and ecstatic, she shouted, "My dear daughter! You are awake at last!"

She kept kissing my hand, forehead, and hair. Her tears wet my face.

"What happened?" I asked again. Each time I tried to open my mouth to speak, I felt pain in my lips.

"Oh, my daughter! How happy I am now! You were asleep for a long time. You were in a coma for six months. You hemorrhaged after delivering the child."

Now I was recalling everything. It seemed as if I was in a nightmare with my eyes open.

"What happened with my child?"

"You calm down first, my daughter! You recover first and then we'll have time to talk."

"Mom! What did they do with my child?"

"What shall I say, dear daughter? They said that the child was born dead," said my mother and continued to kiss my hands.

"No, no! It is not true! I heard, I heard the baby cry! They took my child! I want my child back!" I kept shouting very loudly.

The tubes I had on my arms prevented me from getting up. Mother tried to calm me down.

"What is happening here?" said someone who just entered. He was a new doctor.

"Oh, how great! At last you awoke! My name is Mandi. I am the chief of this pavilion."

"What was done with my child?"

"Listen here! He spoke with a tone of regret. "I have studied your folder. You can't do anything now. Try to get healed and go home. There you have a five-year-old son that waits for you."

"I hate all of you here!" I was speaking with a bitter anger. "You are criminals! One day the law will bring justice and I will fight for my rights. You hear me? All of you are going to end in prison."

"I understand you, I understand." He said this quietly and went out. I remained silent, crying with my face to the wall. My mother tried to tell me what had happened in those six months I was in the coma.

"After you delivered the child, your husband came from Greece. I think he came a month after that. He asked all the doctors and they all gave him the same answer."

"I don't want to hear anymore about him. Where was he when I gave birth to the child? Where was he when I lost my child? Oh, no! Child lost?! I will never accept this! My child is alive! They took him. Someone has paid for my child."

"Calm down, calm down!" said my mother, patting me on the forehead.

During the following days many visitors came to the hospital. Friends and relatives. Some from my husband's family came, too. I was transformed into a tombstone. I did not speak to anybody, though I could hear them all. They were thinking that I had turned into a mad woman. I was not interested in anything at all after this. The only thing I wanted was to see my five-year old son. I wanted to hold him in my arms and pet him endlessly. Oh, how much I was missing him! "Mother, I want to go home. I want to be near my son.""

"Okay, dear," she said, smiling. "Just now I am going to inform them."

Next day I left the hospital. I received hugs and compassion from my husband's people. Perhaps they felt really sorry for me. But to me everything seemed false. And then I saw my son running toward me.

"Mammy, Mammy!" He threw himself into my arms. He stayed like that hugging me for quite a few moments. Then he backed a bit and looked at my hands and belly.

"Mammy, you told me that you would bring me a beautiful baby?"

All those standing around me became silent. Silence! It seemed as if no one was breathing that moment. Two drops slid down my face.

"Yes son. That is so. You are right. It is true that Mammy promised to bring you something special .... from the hospital. A beautiful baby. But the baby became an angel, my dear son! He flew up there. I stretched my hand up toward the sky." He looked for a moment at a small cloud, which, to the surprise of all of us, seemed like an angel.

"I see it, Mammy, I see," shouted the boy happily.

"He sees you, too, my son. He sees and loves you much."

I hugged him and, holding him in my arms, left for home. I did not release him from my arms all the way home. And he, as if understanding me, never asked me to release him. Only when he fell asleep did I put him in his bed.

From the first day after my return home I had many visitors. They expressed their compassion and regret for all what had happened. I could not forget the words of an old woman in her 80s: "Dear daughter, do not hold your head down. I understand your pain, but life continues. You have an excellent boy. He needs you. Do you hear me?"

"Yes, Great Mother."

I answered that way because whoever knew her called her Great Mother. Due to her age, her back was very crooked, even when she walked. She looked like she was carrying a heavy weight on her shoulders. Perhaps one day that weight was going to stop her movement. Nevertheless she said, "... life continues."

I kept looking around the house and everything reminded me of the lost baby: his room that I had prepared for him, his small cotton clothes and blankets, little boy toys I had spread round in the room. The pain was pinching my soul with every passing minute. Where could he be? What happened to him? All these I said loudly. I understood this when my husband said, "It was not in your control what happened. Forget it now!"

I didn't answer him. I had not spoken to him for a long time. He would leave each day at about 8:00 am and return at 10:00 pm. He worked somewhere in a private firm. His brother was his boss.

One day, after they had quarreled with each other, he said, "You were very right. Everything here is in vain. Hopeless. There is no future here. We have to get away. We have to go somewhere where you can forget your pain and I will find our future. Otherwise it will be difficult for us."

I did not speak, but his idea of leaving for somewhere in the West seemed a good idea to me.

"Eh! What do you think?"

"You do what you want," I answered coldly.

Next day he took the money he had saved and went to buy our visa. He returned home very happy, "I got the visas, I got them! Tomorrow we'll go."

And so it happened. I did not refuse at all. I liked the thought that I was going to raise my son in a free world as well as have new possibilities for myself.

And here we were now. The plane took off and we were up in the air. I was looking through the window. My country seemed very small from above. It seemed like a newly built miniature city. And there, on the other side of the sea, we could see Italy stretching out in the shape of a man's boot. Great wonder! It looked so near my country. How was it possible to be so near? How was it possible that they did not let us visit that so beautiful country? The regime had really been very brutal. It had not only caused poverty and pain for the people, but it had kept the Albanian people suppressed and ignorant. Many other people on the plane were speaking about the same things.

"But not anymore," they were saying.

"That regime is already dead now," said a man, who seemed to have suffered much from the communist regime. "But," he added, "you should not forget that we need to work hard to fight old ideas. Many of our parents do not accept new ideas. Perhaps they are not able to understand it."

I was listening to these discussions very attentively. I was feeling glad that at last the revolution we spoke secretly so much about in high school, had now already taken place. Perhaps women would now have the right to free speech and freedom, and become someone in life.

"What are you thinking?" my husband said.

"Nothing," I lied, feeling the red color on my cheeks.

"Eh! I know you well. You think that you are going to do whatever you want in the future? I can cut your head off!" he continued. "Your's and your son's. Did you get me or not? And get me well!"

I understood that this man was never going to change. My thoughts were interrupted by the stewardess, speaking with her beautiful voice:

"Atencione! The plane will be landing soon. Please fasten your seat belts!"

I don't know for how many hours we had been in the air, but now we were landing on an unknown continent in a world that I had heard so much about. In my mind this world was the world of people's dreams. The world of free speech. The world where women like me could come from, after having been locked in an iron cage for years on end. Here we had the possibility of achieving our dreams. This was a world where these iron chains are broken and dreams fly like white doves in search of their favorite place to live.

Welcome to the USA!

I had many emotions. USA! A very big name! My eyes were wet. I happily kissed my son next to me. At last, my son! At last we have arrived! A new big gate opened in front of me! I was looking at everything in astonishment. New York's airport was grandiose. You felt like you were getting lost from moment to moment. But, to my surprise, everything was flowing naturally. After passing through all the check-in formalities, we went out to see the taxis waiting in line.

"Where will you to go!" asked the taxi-driver in broken English, which for us still sounded perfect.

Guessing what the driver asked, my husband said, "To Philadelphia."

Then he showed him the address of a friend who had come here one year ago. I was looking surprised at those big broad streets after coming from the world I had been living until yesterday. Very beautiful, gigantic bridges, huge palaces everywhere! I could not stop looking at them. And, to my surprise, I saw many women driving their cars. My heart was panting hard.

"Maybe, I will one day, too!" "What?" asked my husband as if he was reading my thoughts. "You don't even think about it!"

I turned my head to the window. I already knew that I was going to face a new fight ahead. But I knew at the same time that the strict laws of the American democracy were on my side at any time. And he wouldn't be able to overcome and win over the laws. Never!

In the first days after our arrival we registered in the state offices to receive Social Security numbers, employment authorization, and green cards. Employees in the offices were rather educated. Their English sounded wonderful to my ears. The person who received us accompanied us to all the different offices. These were our first steps. The American state registered us at a free English school, where we could learn English as an important necessity. The school was called DPT. I started studying very seriously and in six months could communicate easily regarding daily matters. The teacher of English, named Peter, was very patient and I tried to be very correct in completing all the grammar work he gave us. When he asked questions, I would only answer if he mentioned my name. This attracted his attention. One day he asked me, "Why do you keep your head down when you answer?"

I didn't know what to tell him. How would he understand the

world I had come from? Or that I had it difficult to communicate with another male, whether he be the teacher of English or someone else. Or, maybe he understood. That I don't know.

"Raise your head when you speak," he said decisively. And while talking, he touched my chin. "Look, just like this!" he said smiling.

My whole body was trembling. What if my husband learned that the teacher had touched me? For sure, he would stop me from going to that school. He himself did not care to come to school. Instead, he started a job in an Italian company named **"Nina Studio."** And he allowed me to attend school on one condition–that I had to go to and come from school every day accompanied by some other women attending that school. This for me was a great step. Only one compatriot woman was in my class, named Ada. She was six years younger than I. Very smart and very beautiful. Once we got to know each other better, I somehow told her about my life. In the end I told her, "Do not hurry to get married! First find the right person and then...."

"Yes, definitely," she said quickly. "Even if you have to fight for your rights. No more old times here. It is a free world." She smiled the simple smile of a child.

"What would you like to become?" she asked me.

"I don't know. I have not even thought about it yet."

"Idiot!" she said. "You may become whatever you want here. You understand? Anything you want!"

"I would love to become a doctor, but this would take me too much time. I like children, too, so I might become a teacher."

Both these professions were related to my idea that I would always be with children. I would take care of them. I would not mind whether the children were white, black, or yellow. My desire was just to be among them and make them smile even a little. If necessary, I wouldn't even mind giving my life for them at any moment. And I would not care whose children they might be.

These thoughts reminded me of my child I had lost. Perhaps my decision to work with children had to do with such past events in my life. After my classes, I was rather joyful. I had a very good schedule in school and had the opportunity of picking up my son on my way home. In the evening I opened the discussion with my husband.

"What if I register in a professional school?"

- "Are you out of your mind?" he asked, furious. "I gave you the maximum freedom by letting you learn the language, and now you even want to become a professional? Huh, what do you want to become?"

"A teacher, or maybe something else," I said fearlessly. "I am going to learn driving, as well. That way I can go to work by myself without anybody's help."

- "Are you crazy, or what ? Who puts these foolish ideas into your head? I can cut your head off! You hear me?" He was growing more heated

"You cannot do anything to me," I said calmly. "Here now we have the laws. You cannot use violence on me anymore. You have done so with me for more than ten years. That is enough now! I don't tolerate injustice anymore! Look around you! Open your eyes and see how much women are progressing here! Turn on the TV and watch Oprah! Isn't she a woman? Look how free she is! Look how much she helps people to go higher in society. Look at Ellen De.... Look..."

"That's enough with these things! Enough! Poor you! Your mind is deceiving you. So, you want to become famous, become a big person, huh? Stop with these foolish ideas. And, if I hear you again, I'll crash your head! You heard me, didn't you?"

I was used to his shouting, and it did not impress me anymore.

"No, I said sharply, "I can't become like them. They are so powerful. But I can become a part of them. To walk on my own feet. To help my family. And why not help others, too? That's what I want, and that's all!"

He approached me, and very angrily said, "Will you shut up, or shall I make you shut up once and forever!"

"I am not afraid of you! I will learn to drive the car and go to work, as well."

He was ready to hit me and stopped one inch away from my face. This world has turned into a true hell!" he whispered and went out, banging the door behind him.

As a matter of fact, I was scared. I didn't actually have to hide it. Each time he would approach me, my body unconsciously shifted to a defensive position. I don't know, but perhaps it had become a necessity from the past. That day he received two shocking blows. One because of my words and the courage I expressed against his will. The next blow was when he went to the club to drink beer with friends. He had heard them discussing the same thing. Two of his compatriot friends, who had long ago come to the U.S., had strongly spoken against all those who did not let their wives learn driving or to go to work. I learned this through their wives, whom I happened to meet accidentally at church. This was a great help to me.

Next day I asked him again, "I will go to get the driver's license? My friend, Ada, will help me with this, too."

"I don't want to hear who you are going with. I will myself come with you."

His answer and reaction surprised me. I did not expect that. In a way he had given in. So the events were rolling fast. I got the driver's license, bought a car and applied for a job in many different places. Soon I received an answer. The first job was in a supermarket. The second was as a nanny in a rich family. I liked to work with children and decided to take that job.

My husband would say, "You must know well that I am going to control you whenever I want."

I did not speak, but inside myself I was happy for making these first steps. I started work immediately and soon I became very good friends with the family and their children. The parents were very friendly and always appreciated the work I was doing for them. I was also happy with the pay and loved the children very much. On the other hand, I felt very tired when I came home after ten hours of work. I had to cook, take care of my son, and everything else in the house. On Saturdays and Sundays I had some time to talk to friends who visited me at home. And they already knew now that my husband did not let me go anywhere. Sometimes I would go to the nearest park to play with my son. He was growing very fast before my eyes and spoke English all the time. This helped me somehow with the new words I had never heard before. He was ten years old now. Often he would join our discussions to give his opinion. So it happened one day when we returned from the park. My husband had come early from work. As soon as he entered the house, he started to yell, "Where have you been?"

"I was playing with our son in the park." I spoke very calmly.

"This means that each time I am not here, you leave the house and wander anywhere you want." Then he came closer to hit me.

The son came close, too, and said, "Hey, what are you doing, Dad? You always get angry without reason. Mom was playing with me." When he finished speaking all that in one breath, he started to cry.

"Don't cry, my dear son, my soul! That's how dad does. He gets angry without reason."

When the son went to bed I went to the kitchen to find my husband drinking beer quietly.

"Never shout at me in front of the son! Okay?"

"What?" he spit out. "You have now even started to raise your voice, too?"

"Yes, I will raise my voice whenever I am right!" I answered.

"Oh, indeed! Here you are, then." Using both his hands he hit me on my cheeks so hard that my eyes were flashing with sparkles. I fell to the floor and stayed like that until I could gather a little strength. After feeling a bit better I tried to get up. My eyes were still cold and I was loaded with anger.

"You have nothing to do with me anymore," I said very decisively.

"I am leaving." I spoke this calmly without any fear, even if I was to die.

"Oh, indeed!" he said again. "If you don't want to see him any-more, then go! While speaking, he grabbed a knife and hurried to the room where the son was sleeping. I will kill you, the son and then my-self. Do you understand that?"

At that moment he had come very close to my son.

"Okay, okay, okay! I will go nowhere! Please, back off from the son!"

He got up with a cunning smile and said, "Like this, yes! Like this you become a good woman, huh! Come on now, to the room!"

And, dragging me forcefully, threw me on the bed just like a paper doll. I looked through the window and saw the raindrops hit inces-santly against the window that had already turned gray. Thunder and lightning in the sky looked like nature trying to light everything on fire. Mother nature seemed to be very furious. My skin was shrinking, or at least, it seemed so to me. The rain did not stop for a long time. I found myself hunched in a corner of the room deep in thought. How could I go to work like this with bruised and swollen eyes? How would I explain all this to them? For a moment I directed my eyes to the bed where he was comfortably sleeping after having beaten me physically and morally. A frightening thought flared up my mind. What if I take my son and leave right now at night? But where to go? He will be able to find me. Oh, no! I am not going to play with the life of my son! I went up and slept next to my son.

Next morning, after sending my child to school, I went to work. None asked me about my bruised eyes. I even tried to avoid others. By the end of the day, before leaving for home, my boss asked me, "Are you okay? Is there anything I can do for you?"

At that moment she seemed to be my closest friend. I hugged her and said, "Maybe one day I am going to talk to you."

She smiled and said, "Okay. And promise me you will do that, okay?"

- "Alright," I said and hugged the children I was taking care of. After that I added,

"Good night, my loves!" They both threw themselves on my arms and said, "No, don't go, please! It is still early."

"I will come back," I said, caressing their small lovely heads, smelling the shampoo scent mixed with children's sweetness.

While driving home I was thinking again. How is it possible that unknown people can become so respectful and lovable? And, on the other hand, the person whom I had already served for many years, not only didn't show any gratitude at all, but was using violence against me. I had already come to the point of not wanting to return home again. The only thing that made me do so was my son.

And on the way home I was still wondering: how would it be possible that I one day could become free like all the American women? Free to study, free to speak and express my thoughts and ideas? And why not free to go to the stores and buy a pair of shoes, something that was impossible without his permission? Now I was beginning to understand that it was not enough simply living in a democratic country to be free. No, you had to fight even with that person you are living with, who does not accept democracy at all. In his spirit and mind that man was still 100% old fashioned and with dictatorial conviction. But, how many women were suffering from this in my country? Thousands. The youth of that country subdued the communist system. But it was difficult to subdue the dictatorial ideas in people's minds. You had to fight a war the end of which no one knew. It was a real battle—a war with my own husband. He was allowed to do whatever he wanted. To go out whenever he wanted. To come back home whenever he wanted. But me, no! I was not allowed to ask him where he had been.

I had recently noticed that he not only had doubled his time away, but time and again I smelled perfume fragrances. And it may seem strange, but I didn't feel at all jealous. I had completely lost any interest in him and his actions. But within me I was thinking and drew the conclusion that he had lost interest in working and this meant that he was having fun somewhere, but I didn't know where. If I managed to catch him red-handed, I would have the right to raise my voice. And so I did.

One day, as on every other morning, I made my son ready and sent him to school. My husband rested assured that I went to work. In fact, I phoned my work place and asked for a day off. When I returned home, his car was still there. My heart started to beat heavily. What would I tell him if everything was okay? Well, maybe I'd tell him that I was not feeling well. I stopped talking to myself, breathed in deeply, and pushed the car door open. I walked slowly to the house entrance, opened the door silently, placed the keys on the table near me, and looked around. Nothing. What an idiot I was! I decided to leave without being noticed. Suddenly a light noise in the beginning became clearer with every moment. That noise was coming from the room upstairs. A woman's groaning voice mixed with the voice of a man! At the beginning some ehs and ohss by her and then his obscene voice saying, "That's it bitch, oh, go ahead, push more! That's it! ..." He didn't stop saying dirty words.

It was more than clear and despicable. Very quietly I sat on the chair and said, I'm a moron. How on earth didn't I think about such a thing earlier? But, what now? I spoke to myself again. What would I do? He never let's me do anything. He will kill me before I do anything! My thoughts were intermixing with their ugly sex. However, I had to prove to him that he is nothing more than dirty dung. A dirty creature. He did not deserve a family, though he kept it through violence.

I stood up walking back and forth, and accidentally my foot hit the chair, which fell over, making a noise. My God! What would happen now?

He came down instantly half naked. When he saw me, his face went completely white, "Oh! It's you! Why did you come back?" He was looking at me spitefully.

"You do not deserve an answer! But I am telling you: This is my home. You and she, the other one, go and find another dirty toilet! You don't have a place here anymore!"

That other one came quickly down, holding half of her clothes in her hand.

"Make me a phone call," she shouted while leaving the house. He didn't dare to turn his head to her.

"Since when are you like this?" he asked me surprised. "Since when have you become so wise and strong?" While talking, he was approaching me. I went a few steps backward toward the kitchen and grabbed a knife quickly. "Don't come any closer!" I shouted with all the strength I had within me.

He was frozen, but did not show his fear. "Come on!" he said. "Make no jokes! Let's finish together what I started with her."

Oh God! Hatred and disgust mixed together within my being! I felt like throwing up. "You have no human personality at all! You really need help! You are very sick, indeed. You need therapy. Just go for it wherever you can. I will never live with you anymore! You hear me? Never!" I held the knife in my hand all the time. I was trembling all over from fear. "Get out of here!" I shouted again.

"Okay, okay! Stop now," he said when he saw that I was not going to surrender this time.

"Give me time–a few hours. I must meet the son and take something, too. Please!" he said, moving away.

I breathed in deeply and, like an idiot, said okay. "You have three hours only. If I find you here again when I come home, then I will call the police. You got me?"

"Yes, I got you," he said and threw himself on the couch. Then he got up and took a bottle of whiskey in his hand. He was guzzling it. I went out, slamming the door behind me. For the first time in my life I felt myself freed from a very heavy burden weighing on me all entire life. I jumped into my car, but where to go? After a moment's smile, I repeated: To the mall, the block of stores. When I turned the engine on, a song from the radio echoed in my ears:

I like to move it, move it; you like to move it…

I didn't change the station as before. On the contrary, I increased the volume and joined the radio singing, too. I had already made about two miles when I noticed that I was feeling joyous. For the first time I had raised my voice against an injustice. How easy it had been! I saw now what a true idiot I had been! Why had I not raised my voice before? But wait! What was I saying? Who would let me? None would give me right. Above all I was a woman. Nobody would accept the divorce. None would say, "She is right." If I would have done the same thing back in my country, I would have been punished and blamed and shamed forever. And not only that, but most of the people there would call me different insulting names, like "whore, prostitute; she did not stay with her husband. She just only wants to wander around." Who knows what else they would have said against me. And that is why women there accept the violence levied on them by men.

"That's enough! Stop it!" I shouted as if I was in front of them. "Raise your voice! I did and am feeling very good now. I feel free."

I parked the car somewhere, and remained for some moments in the car just to take a deep breath after all that talking to myself. What was going to happen with me? I kept walking through that wide walkway of the mall. My eye caught a beauty shop on the right side of the walkway and I went in with slow steps.

"Welcome!" said a sympathetic lady with ruffled loose hair, which was considered then to be the fashion in town.

"What are you going to do today with your hair?" she asked me, leading me to the chair where I should sit.

"Everything," I answered decisively. "I have time to do all, my hair, nails, everything. Or, better, I leave it up to you; you may do anything you want with me today."

After I finished talking, I rested my head on the chair and took a deep breath again.

"You must have a special reason, I believe?" she asked me.

After a long pause, I said, "Yes, I won my freedom today."

She smiled, but did not ask any further. The warm water was flow-ing through my hair. Oh! What a pleasure! I was feeling the scent of shampoo and the hair-dresser's hands giving the massage. Oh, how stupid I have been! I was thinking once more. Why didn't I try this before? I was really feeling good. I forgot who I was. I left myself in the hands of that woman who was moving her hands quickly from one to the other side of my head. She gave my hair a chestnut color and a bit of reddish shade. Then she cut and combed it very carefully.

"Yes, do you like it?"

I saw myself in the mirror. "I am liking it very much," I answered.

"We are not done yet," she said again. "Put your feet here! While I take care of your face, someone else will take care of your feet and hands. I did not refuse. And I don't know how much time I spent there. But when I left, I realized that three whole hours had passed.

"Have fun!" rang the voices of the girls behind me who took care of me. I bid farewell to them with my hand. Oh, how well I was feel-ing! I had never felt like that before. I passed two more hours shop-ping here and there in different stores of the mall. And why should I lie? I did hear some compliments. Then I thought it was time to go home. But first I had to pass by the school to pick up my son. Definitely I had to explain to my son why his father had left. Oh, how happy I was! My son saw the car in line with the other cars and ran toward me.

"Mammy!" he called.

"Mammy's soul! Come on! Let's go to our home."

"Okay, Mammy, let's go."

I had bought many things for him like toys, books, and different sweets. In the meantime he was asking: What is this? What is that?

Instead of answering, I let him open everything first. Usually when

I bought something for him, he had to wait to open it until arriving home.

"But today we broke the rules!" he said surprised.

"Starting from today we shall have new rules." While talking I was laughing and he looked at me surprised.

"Okay," he said, and his grin turned into a laugh, too. "Since we are breaking the rules, let's stop here for an ice-cream!" he said, suddenly playful.

I saw him in the mirror. His face seemed to say - please!

"Why not?" I said, and we stopped at Rita's store. There we enjoyed Rita's Water-ice and playing with each other. At the beginning he wanted to try the taste of Mango ice cream. Just to joke with him, I opened my mouth and tried to get the ice cream he was licking. To avoid this he began running around saying: "No, no!"

Oh, how happy he was! However, I wasn't sure which one of us was happier at this moment. I was thinking about this as I pampered my son.

For some moments I had already forgotten that we had to return home. I looked at my watch and told him, "Let's go now," He did not refuse and stretched his hands to mine. His face had some spots of ice cream. "My soul!" I spoke to him while cleaning his face. "I have something else to give you…."

"Ohh! How fun!" he interrupted. "Another surprise?"

"No, no! Listen to me now!" At that moment we had entered the car. "Now you are grown enough. My whole life has been a sacrifice only for you. I have always thought of you and tried to make sure you get raised as well as possible. Now that you are grown I want to tell you that me and your father do not get along well. So today we decided to separate. But this does not mean that you will not see him anymore. He is your father. You will be free to go and spend time with him whenever you want."

In the quietest way possible he asked. "Have you talked to father about these things?"

His calmness surprised me. He looked me straight into my eyes and said, "Why, do you think that I don't understand you? You always quarrel. But I don't want you to leave each other. He will get very angry. Who knows what he might do?"

These words he said very quickly, fearing that I might interrupt him. The answer of my son made me open my mouth in surprise. He might be right.

"Now it's already decided. I spoke to him this morning. I made this decision due to some events that took place this morning. When you grow older I will explain it better to you."

I turned on the car engine and glanced at him in the mirror. His eyes had become wet. He turned his head to the window. I understood at once that he did not like this. Eh! Who is that child that can easily accept his parents' separation? In the meantime, while approaching our home, my heart began beating heavily. What if he was still there? How would I act? I parked the car and breathed in deeply. My son did not wait. He got out of the car and said, "Come on! What are you waiting for?" Without thinking anymore, I pushed the car door open. As soon as I entered the house, I sensed a heavy aroma. An alcohol scent mixed with vomit. Oh, my God! What had happened here! Two meters away from me I saw my husband lying on the floor with his arms stretched out. Next to him on the floor I saw two empty bottles of whiskey.

Without thinking any further I took my son in my arms, while he cried, "Daddy, Daddy! Get up, Daddy!"

I ran to the phone and dialed 911. The ambulance came within minutes. But those minutes to me seemed interminable. My son escaped my embrace and ran up to his room crying. I heard his trembling voice, "Do you see what you have done? Do you?"

I was totally lost. "What should I do?"

I let the son go upstairs to his room and did not answer him. Very scared, I turned around and touched my husband to find a pulse. People rushed out of the ambulance, immediately entered the house, and were asking me the routine questions. While they were trying to bring him back to life, I was completely frozen. I heard somebody say, "He is alive, he is alive! Hurry up with the oxygen."

After some minutes they left together with his body in a stretcher. Though the ambulance had left, two police cars were still there.

"Lady, lady! Can you tell us, please, what happened here?"

Actually I could not speak, as I was trembling all over. The police threw a blanket over my shoulders. "Lady, calm down! Your husband is in safe hands. Now he is out of danger. Do you hear me, lady?"

"My son, my son!" I spoke like a crazy lady. "My son!"

"Lady, where is your son?"

I pointed out with my finger: upstairs!

He ran upstairs and I heard these words: "Your father will be okay. Calm down now!"

"Okay!" I heard the weak voice of my son. His voice was followed by a sigh. They came downstairs and my son ran to me as soon as he saw me. I hugged him tightly without saying any word at all. I was completely stiffened and didn't know what to say.

"Okay, lady! Now you have to answer some questions. This is part of the routine investigation."

- "Alright," I said.

"What happened here and how?"

"But I don't know how," I said in a trembling voice. In the morning I talked to my husband about divorce...." I continued to tell everything that had happened with me. My son heard the whole story, too. He did not leave me for a second.

After I finished telling everything, I understood what I had done. Somehow I was the reason that he had tried to kill himself. He had not accepted the possibility of separating from me. He would better accept death instead. I am not able to express what sort of emotions I was going through those moments. This was unjust. Not just at all.

Ohh! My God! What shall I do? What must I do now? I had tried to undertake a step that seemed just to me for the first time. As a matter of fact, I was completely paralyzed now. I don't know for how long I had been sitting stooped on the couch. I opened my eyes and tried to release my hand from under my son's head and put a pillow there instead. I looked at him for a long time. My son! Your Mom hurt your soul unwittingly. After I covered him with a warm blanket, I put some water to boil for making some warm tea as a tranquillizer. Oh! How much I needed to have someone near me now! My mother or one of my sisters. But all were too far away. My thoughts were interrupted by a phone call. I was scared.

"Hello! Yes, please!"

"We are calling from the hospital, maam. Your husband is out of danger now. He is going to be well. We have to keep him for another day or more in the hospital. You may visit him whenever you want. Do you hear me?"

"Yes, yes. Thank you," I answered and hung up. Now everything was more than clear. He would come back home. I had no choice.

But what if I informed his relatives to take him home and take care of him? No, no! This was impossible. They were too far away, beyond the Atlantic Ocean. No, indeed. This was quite impossible. Last of all, what was their fault? I was feeling that the whole world was rotating in front of my eyes. To me it seemed that it was the end of my life.

But, no! This was not the end of the world. That was my end. I had no other way out. If I divorced him, he would kill himself. And my son would hate me for the rest of my life. Ow! How much had I tortured myself with such questions when I was only talking and talking to myself about separating from him! And what now? Now it was more than clear. A stony wall was raised in front of me. And exactly in front of that wall was placed the picture of my son! Dare and play that game if you want! It seemed as if that wall was declaring: You are playing with the life of your son! He will hate you, he will hate you!

I was sitting on the cold floor of the kitchen. My buttocks had become dull cold. Suddenly someone knocked on the door. It was my neighbor. I had already shared many things with her before. She was a woman almost in her seventies. I used to call her Nona. As soon as I saw her, I threw myself in her arms. "Nona! Oh, how much I need you!"

She hugged me very emotionally and said, "I saw the ambulance and the police. What happened here? I was so concerned and wanted to come and see you."

"Oh, Nona! How great that you came! I am losing my mind."

After we sat down, tea cups in hand, I explained to her in every detail what had happened. She was listening and shaking all over. She was the only person in the USA, who, more or less, knew my life. She was the only person who had seen the bruises on my body caused by the violence he had perpetrated on me. She was the only person who was able to understand me.

"I feel very sorry, very sorry!" she said when I stopped speaking. "This is not just at all," she continued. "By doing this he has shown himself to be very weak and peevish. Weak, selfish and unjust. And what about your son? How is he doing?"

"He was scared to death. Such a thing had never crossed my mind. It was the first time in my life that it seemed to me I had made a momentous correct decision. For the first time in my life I felt free. But still it didn't depend on me. My decision was almost killing him. And now, what? What must I do? I kept talking and talking. Nona saw that I was in complete depression.

"Calm down!" she said to me. "In fact, all this he has done is very unjust. Many women would say: 'Very bad for you, dear husband!' and they would continue their normal life. And this is more than right," she continued breathing deeply. "But I know you well. You would never do that. As a matter of fact you are feeling guilty about everything that happened, isn't it so?"

I raised my head surprised. "Yes," I said. This woman had a very special virtue. She could completely empathize.

"I want to give you a piece of advice about what you must do," she continued after a pause. "But this is only up to you. Nonetheless, you have faith in God. He is with you at all times. Speak to Him! I am very sure that you will find a way out of this situation. These things I had to tell you." Then she hugged me again. Her eyes were wet with tears.

After Nona left, I took some old pictures in my hand. I began looking at them one by one. There was my whole life. My son's life, too. Oh, how much these pictures were speaking to me! A fake smile here and there. I threw them to the middle of the room. They looked like worn-out fragments of paper, pieces of which put back together would not have any meaning. I raised my head upward.

Great God! Why so? Please give me an answer! Why did You abandon me? In the beginning I lost my first love. Then my child, my hardly born angel. And now You've blocked each step, each movement. Please, speak to me! The only love I have is my son. Only he is left to me. I don't want to lose him. Great God! Please stay with me!

After these prayers and cries I felt completely exhausted. I threw myself on the couch. I was an idiot. A true idiot! I closed my eyes.

Where are you, my Father? I wondered. It is not that I have forgotten you. Not a single moment! What am I wanting now? I must have guidance. With my eyes closed, I heard my son's steps. I didn't open my eyes. "I am here, Mom, I am here."

He held my hands and said, "Stand up, Mom! Stand up!"

I stood up, hugging him tightly with all my strength.

"Where to go, my son?"

- "Anywhere," he answered.

All my terrible thoughts fled at that moment. And, hugging him tightly, I looked through the window. Blocks of clouds were moving away. Little by little I could see the blue and endless sky.

"Okay son, let's go!"

Walking outside we felt the fresh air caressing our faces. I breathed deeply lost in thought. My son was growing up so fast! So beautiful, so amazing!

Part
Two

The Dream

"Please, tell me what happened next," my friend kept asking me eagerly.

Her name was Melina. She was tall and her short hair gave her the appearance of a sportswoman. Her blue eyes shone when speaking. She had two daughters. She was a dedicated mother and woman to her family. My acquaintance with her happened normally. I was working near her home. My boss was good friends with Melina. She often asked to learn about me, and so did I about her. I liked her as a person and she seemed to match perfectly with my type. And maybe, due to this, we grew closer to each other.

She interrupted my thoughts. "Come on, tell me please!"

"What shall I tell you? The last event with my husband paralyzed me. I felt totally blocked. What could I do next? I felt like an island where there is neither entrance nor exit."

While speaking to her, I kept my head down, not to let her see my wet eyes.

"Still I will try to do something for myself."

"Come on, speak because now you've brought the smile back to my face," she said, laughing.

"I am going to start school. In that way I will not have time to think much."

"What are you going to study?"

"Medicine, I would like."

"Oh, that's so great! And I know that you are going to succeed."

I thanked her with a warm hug. She understood that I didn't want to talk any further, and stood up to go. "As a matter of fact, sometime I would like to hear more about Arbi," she said, waving her index finger. As soon as I heard mention of his name a broad smile lightened my face.

After that I pulled myself together and answered, "I don't know what to say. For me it is simply a dream. And surely he has got his own family now and perhaps doesn't remember or think about me at all. It's likely so, my dear."

After I finished talking, I saw her off at the main entrance.

"I will come back again," she said with a grin. "In the meantime you take care of yourself."

I said, "You have become to me like Curious George."

I closed the door and took a deep breath.

I have more than enough worries to care about. These words I was speaking to my logic, but my heart would not obey me. It turned me back to the same point. My love! A dream that pops up and disappears. Appears again and again. And I was not able to touch that dream with snipped or paralyzed wings. How is it possible?! I wondered. You keep your most beautiful dream within yourself. As a matter of fact, you live with it. And that beautiful dream never leaves you. It becomes your inseparable part in eternity. It's a wonder !

Days were passing fast, and here at last, the first day of school came. To return to school at age forty is not easy, I was thinking, while walking along the corridors of that big building. I had a little fear within me. But this was only for the first few days. When I became a bit better acquainted and somehow comfortable with the subjects, I was feeling rather good. All the medical terms actually were in Greek or Latin languages. This somehow was simpler for me compared to the American students because my ears were used to the foreign languages. The only difficulty I was facing was the computer. While the other students would complete their programs within an eye's wink, I would always be the last to finish. But soon I could get the upper hand of this situation, too. The American girls in my class were rather friendly and always ready to help. So I was developing a sort of pride for being able to complete these studies at my age.

My husband now was not reacting as he did before. He was trying not to intervene—trying to convince me that he had already changed. However, it was very tiring to cover all bases: school, work and family. The work, specifically, was a great responsibility. To work as a nanny with three small children was rather tiring. I not only had to be skillful and physically strong, but had to also be patient and careful in the process of educating them. In fact I was feeling lucky as the parents of these children were highly educated and I had become very friendly with them. I loved the kids so much. This helped me not get bored and do everything with enthusiasm. The three little girls I was taking care of were all blonde and had blue eyes. It was normal to get rather tired but each time I returned home from work I would carry with me the love of these children—a love without conditions, and their smiles made me forget everything else.

However, it did not end with this. The work, school, ...and the family needed their time. At midnight the book I was reading, would fall on my face as I drifted to sleep. Still I would get up and tell myself : there is no other way but waking up! As a matter of fact, being so busy, I had somehow won a certain comfort. It was important at that time that my son be raised with all the best things and that I not be an obstacle to his future. He, too, had been tired enough seeing and watching our endless quarrels. Now it was his turn—his time--to enjoy every happy moment. He had grown a lot. On weekends I had more time to take care of him. I would cook his favorite foods. And he liked my care but often would say, "Mom, I am a man now. I can take care myself." He was changing a lot. Most of the time he would stay with his friends outside. He was even somehow distancing himself from me. There were cases when he returned home late at night, and often would not answer his cell phone, either.

"At least answer your cell phone when I call you, my son! Just tell me where you are going and when you will return home."

"Mom! Enough! What do you want, to control my life? Let me do wrong things. Let me learn from them." After that he would just leave very irritated.

Buuut... I was not at all prepared at this age. I didn't know how to act. I was only speaking to him with the instinct of a mother. Every night I would pray to God: "Please, God : guard my son and the sons of all mothers from evil!"

Every day, when he went out, he would say, "Mom! I am going out now."

"Wait!" I'd call and I would run after him. "Get your jacket; it is cold outside. And don't be late, please! Who will you go out with? Where will you go?"

"Mom! Enough, you are tiring me!"

He would leave in haste, and I, silently, used to say my prayer: "May God protect you, my son!"

Days like this would follow thereafter. Each time he went out my worries became more serious. Such a thing happened one evening. It was Friday. After I returned home from work I greeted my son and asked him, "What do you say, would you like to go out with me to-night and have dinner somewhere?"

"What are you saying, Mom? I will go out with my friends."

"You may go out with your friends tomorrow. Tonight let's go out together, please!"

"I will go with my friends. Period!"

I heard my husband from the living room, "But why don't you let him do whatever he wants? He is grown up now." I went close to him and, in a lower voice, told him, "Are you not concerned that he is staying outside at night? Your negligence really inflames me."

"But he is grown now, and it is his time to go through such things. As a matter of fact, I like that he wants to go out. I need some privacy, too."

I looked at him for a second while he was preparing his preferred drink then turned my back to him. The thought that my son was doing something wrong would never leave my mind. I turned around once again to my husband and said, "Please, communicate with him! Maybe he needs to speak to someone."

"You are acting strange! He doesn't even say hello or goodbye to me."

"Well, just go once and see who he goes with and what he does."

"What?! No! I won't do that. Now let him do whatever he wants."

Our conversation was interrupted by the cell phone. "Hello Mammi! I will come home late tonight. Don't wait for me. We are going to celebrate the birthday of a friend."

"But where is the address you are going to be?" I asked immediately. "Oh, come on Ma, what are you saying! I have to go now, we'll speak later."

"Wait, I ....." but there was only a beep...beep...beep . I said, "I love you" anyway! My word love came out with a long deep sigh, as if to say why, why my dear son? With slow steps I went into his room. I sat at his computer desk, grabbed a white piece of paper and began to write:

"My dear son! Never forget! Whatever you will do, right or wrong, nothing changes how much I

love you! I feel it deep in my heart that you will become the best of the best. It's only this I live for. My life would not have any meaning if I did not see you happy. I will be by your side at every moment. Wherever you will go or whatever you do, never forget your mom's advices. Open your eyes and see! You are surrounded by my love! I love you so much!"

Your Mother

I put my letter on his notebook, set some clothes in order in his room and went to my room to pray for him as I always did before sleeping. To sleep in this situation was like lying on thorns. Now and then I would get up and go to see if my son had come home. My eyes, tired and heavy, were closed and passed into another world. Confused dreams, mixed faces, known and unknown to me. Different voices, all kinds of noises, and then silence. Deep in that silence clear smooth voices were heard: "Get up, don't sleep!"

I tried to open my eyes, but couldn't. Voices continued again: get up, what are you waiting for?

"Who is speaking? What has happened?"

Two white angels appeared somehow in a cloud.

"Your son is in danger. You must go now!"

The cloud little by little became clearer and I opened my eyes to see who was speaking. In my dark room only my husband's snoring was heard.

What was this strange dream ?! I jumped out of bed and dialed my son's cell phone. It was shut off. I saw it was 2:00 a.m.

"Enough with that noise now! I have worked all day and want to sleep," yelled my husband.

"You must get up," I told him. "I have seen a very terrifying dream.

Go and find your son! Please!"

"What? You may go if you want. I cannot."

I knew that I was wasting time with him. I threw my dressing gown over my shoulders and went out straight to the car. But where could I go? I felt like I was going crazy. The dream and the night's darkness plunged me into a more terrible fear.

I didn't know how long I drove through different narrow neighborhood streets of the town before the police stopped me.

"Where are you going, lady? You are driving the wrong way on a one-way street."

"I apologize, but I didn't see that. I am looking to find my son. He does often come to this neighborhood." My lips were trembling. I didn't know whether it was the cold or the fear.

"I don't know how to help you, but I do know that there was a party for many hours on the other side of the street. Somebody had his birthday. But now that neighborhood has become quiet. However, you can go and try to ask there." The officer stopped talking and was looking at me with pity. "You give me the name and phone number of your son. In the meantime we can also search for him. If we find him we'll let you know. How old is he? ""Is he over 18 years old." I said yes in a low voice.

"Lady, then you'd better return home. Your son will return home himself."

I started the car again and headed to the address the police told me of. On the other side of the street not the slightest sound was heard. and there was nothing to be seen. I was looking around desperately. Somewhere I saw a light on in one house. Maybe there! My heart was beating fast. I approached that house and got out of the car leaving the engine on. I knocked on the door, "Is anybody here?" Silence. "I am looking for my son, please! Tell me something about him." Silence again. I started to tremble even more. The cold and fear had penetrated deep into my spinal cord. I must find him! I definitely must find him.

What was that dream? I felt like crying loudly. I made a movement to return to my car. At that moment I stepped on the belt of my gown and fell on the cold concrete stairs. I didn't feel any pain but seemed frozen. My right foot seemed to be heavier. In the quietness of that cold night I had the visual image of a dead person. When I was close to my car I turned my head once more to look around. On the left side of the house my eye caught something at the stairs of the next building. There I saw a man lying on those stairs. My God! I screamed . Oh, no! Not in this cold. "Hey, you man!" The temperature maybe was much below zero at this time of the night.

"Hey there!" I shouted. "Wake up! You will freeze here!"

I went closer to him and touched his shoulder. The smell of alcohol was strong as soon as I came very close to him. ! I raised my voice a little. "What is wrong with you?" Nothing. No answer at all. I shook him and tried to move him around so as to see his face. Terrified, I immediately stood up. "My son! My son!"

I glanced around. Help! Nothing. Darkness! I put my two hands on his face. "Wake up, son, wake up! You are frozen."

I took off my gown and covered him in the hope of warming him up somehow. Oh, God! He's breathing! I was so happy and kissed his forehead, his eyes and his face. I tried to lift him, but it was impossible. I grabbed him by the arms and pulled him toward the car. I put him inside and turned the heater to maximum. His eyes were tightly shut as if somebody had sewn them.

"Come on a little farther, come on!" I was I talking to myself. All my talking right then was actually desperate prayer—prayer all mixed with my broken voice and tears. "A little longer son, your mother's heart!" Lights of my car penetrated the freezing darkness. I don't know how many minutes had elapsed before I found myself in front of my house. I left the car running, hurried inside and screamed, "Get up and help me!"

My husband came out terrified. We put him inside. I was still talking to myself : my soul, my heart! I quickly got some warm water and a towel and began to warm up his face and hands. He was still asleep. That way talking to myself I had fallen asleep next to him. My lips had touched his forehead. When I opened my eyes the sun had already spread whiteness and light everywhere, though still cold, very cold. My son continued to sleep. In the meantime I prepared some tea and hot soup. Then I waited and waited for him to wake up. I grabbed his hands lightly and murmured: "Wake up son!" He was warm and still sleeping as if for a whole week he had not slept at all. Thinking and caressing his forehead softly, hours had passed and I had fallen asleep again. I don't know how much time had elapsed the moment I opened my eyes. I was looking around rubbing my eyes. My son was awake now and I threw my eyes toward the sky, and silently said: "Thank you God!" In silence again I hugged my son.

"I stood up, warmed up the soup and brought two bowls, one for each.

"Eat, my soul, while the soup is warm."

"Hey there, do you see what you did to your mother?" said my husband.

My son was sipping the warm soup.

"What kind of a son are you? Say it!"

My son put the spoon down, raised his head and, looking at my husband, spoke, "Why don't you tell me what kind of a husband you are? Tell me what kind of a man on earth lets his wife go out alone in the middle of a freezing night?"

Silence prevailed in the kitchen. Only the sound of our two spoons touching the soup bowls could be heard. At that moment I looked up at my son and spoke, "Eat a little more, please!" He, too, looked straight into my eyes. Then he hung his head and said, "Mom, forgive me, please!"

I took his hand and kissed him. "The most important thing is that you are well now."

He pulled me to himself and decisively said, "I swear, Mom ! Everything is going to be back in order."

His lips rested on my forehead. In the middle of his kisses he kept murmuring, "My mother! My mother!"

I did not ask him any questions. Neither did he tell me anything. But that moment told me a lot. It was a moment that is engraved and remains within you for the rest of your life. After this event my son did not go out late anymore, he was communicating more…but I never learned what he drank that night. I knew that this one night, glimpsing my son lying face down on those steps covered with ice, would remain in my mind forever, like a bad picture that you cannot burn. My son had now started to take rather good care of himself after what had happened. We would converse longer with each other. And what I liked best was the Friday nights when we would go out to have dinner together. Sometimes we even watched movies together.

My school year was coming to an end. I really needed some rest. And what if I went to Europe after school? It would be a very beautiful thing, indeed, if my son came with me. It was a long time we had not seen our parents and sisters. And I mentioned this idea to my son in the evening.

"And why not?" was his answer. "But you know that I have no money for vacations." "I know." I laughed with all my heart. "But this time I will cover your trip."

"I will come, too," said my husband.

We did not speak. We shrugged our shoulders as if to say to him: do whatever you want.

School would come to an end in two months time but I reserved the tickets without thinking long term. "Two months will pass soon," I told my son. "In the meantime we can prepare ourselves for the trip. We may buy some presents for grandma and grandpa. What do you say?"

With a sly smile, he said, "I will be the most beautiful present for them. But for you, yes, you need some presents for them." I laughed, too, but asked him, "What do you mean when you say that?"

He put his two fingers over his eyebrows and made the gesture that meant,' I am very handsome.' I shook my head in disagreement, and added, "You are liking yourself too much. Don't forget that our feet walk on the ground and not in the air!"

He laughed. "Come on, Mom, I keep my feet on the ground." He bowed his head as if in deep humility. "Are you happy now?" He laughed.

"Yes, very much so." I went close to him and gave him a hug. Ooooh, how tall he had become! Then, pleased with this, I picked up the phone to give my family back home the good news that we were going there for vacation.

"Let's get all together once more just like we were long ago."

All were very happy with this news. My youngest sister said, among other things,

"When you come I have a nice surprise for you."

"What is it? Please tell me!"

"No, not now. Not til you get here. You have to just wait till then. Okay?" And she laughed.

At last the day of our departure came. How fun! I would stay one full month there. I had planned two weeks with the family and two more weeks at the beach. Beaches in Europe are fantastic. But my birthplace had magic bathing beaches, as well. Besides that, the traditional cooking was a dream come true. For about five years I had not gone on vacations at all. And now, when thinking of this trip, the clean air of the Ionian Sea and the fine sands of the beaches were back in my imagination.

My husband did not oppose this decision. He only put a condition on the trip. In the beginning we had to visit his family in compliance with the old Albanian tradition.

"Then," he added, "you may go to your family and to the beach because I have my plans, too, while you are away."

He was waiting for my reaction but I did not go against it at all.

"Yes, I agree with that." I spoke calmly and within myself I was feeling rather satisfied for the fact that I was going to enjoy these days with my son and my family alone.

I was reveling in beautiful emotions during the whole trip back home. During the first days I was with his family and tried to be as calm as possible. However, there was a moment when my mother-in-law noticed my attitude and she told this to her son, "She seems to be quite indifferent this time!"

"No, why do you say that? We are quite alright," said my husband. Then he looked at me as if to say, "Can't you speak up a little?"

"I am asking you because they say that there in America everything is done the way women want" my mother-in law said after a short pause. "But here it doesn't work like that!" Her voice was going higher. "Here," she continued, "if females raise their voices, the club hits their backs."

My youngest sister-in-law was looking straight into my eyes. With that look I knew what she was saying: "Speak, don't remain silent on this topic."

"Well, what do you think?" I spoke without raising my voice. "Is it right to use violence on females like a century ago? Is this humane? What about your daughters? Would it hurt you if they were beaten like that? Nobody has the right to use violence against anybody else." After these words I took a deep breath and felt somehow released. I walked away from them, leaving mother and son to discuss it between themselves. My sister-in-law came to join me on the veranda outside.

"Blessed be your mouth!" she said. "I want to speak too, but I can't. I fear that my husband will beat me." Then she asked me, "Shall I make a coffee for you?"

"Thank you, but I will make some coffee for both of us," I said with a smile.

I had a good time with my sisters-in-law and their children. With the rest I kept some distance.

Those first days seemed rather long to me. I eagerly waited to go and meet my own relatives.

"I will drive you," said my husband. "I will rent a car and accompany you."

"No problem," me and my son answered at the same time.

On the way home I was looking at each and every small street with much fond yearning. My mother and sisters received us very warmly. Oh, how good I felt to be among them! How much I had missed them! My husband stayed with us that night and the next day returned to his relatives. It was the first time that we were having a vacation each on our own. Maybe it doesn't sound right to say it but I enjoyed it more without him. I needed so much to have quiet time to clear my mind. Days with my family members were great, noisy and filled with activity. My son was having a lot of fun. He had many cousins his age and I was very comfortable as they did their own thing. Girls of the neighborhood kept staring at him and whispering. He obviously liked to have the attention of those people around him. I felt so safe that he was surrounded by my relatives. In the end, what disaster can happen to you when you are surrounded by your own people that you know intimately? At most he might like some girl there. And this would not be a bad thing.

In the midst of my thoughts I heard my sister's voice. It was my youngest sister. She had told me that she had a surprise for me. But what was that?

"Are you ready?" she said.

"Give me a hint first," I answered.

"Can you figure out who I am talking about? Do you know who asks about you all the time?"

"You are really confusing me," I said. "Whoever is asking about me at this age must be crazy."

"Yes," she answered quickly, "that might be so for you!"

"Enough with the silliness. Tell me what you have to tell." She was staring at me smiling, but did not speak yet.

I raised my voice. "Come on, speak up!"

She only uttered one word. "Arbi!".

My mouth remained half open.

"Arbi?" I squeaked. "How is he? What is he doing? Whom does he live with?" I knew I was blushing shamelessly.

My sister laughed loudly. "Wait a little, calm down. Breathe deep!" She started making fun of me. I ignored her sarcasm and continued, "Is he okay? Tell me!"

"But be patient first," said my sister. "By the way, he has never married."

"What?"

"Yes, one hundred per cent true! He went through a very bad time after your marriage," continued my sister. "Many girls tried to enter into relations with him but he never had any interest in a serious relationship. And he still does not want to get married."

My sister's facial expression was telling me something. Her big eyes were expressing joy, as if she was telling me of a miracle. I was frozen. I did not know how to continue with this conversation. My brain was trying to show some restraint. My heart was doing the contrary, beating faster and faster. All this confusion in my whole body made me speak meaningless words out of my mouth. "No.... but ..... why...."

"What?" asked my sister. Her clear voice brought me back to myself. I know my appearance betrayed me. After I could speak some sense, I said, "Why do I have to know what he is doing? Tell me why?"

"No, no, just thought you'd like to know...," laughed the sister and went out, leaving me alone in that electrified room. The truth is I had never forgotten him, but was afraid to find out how he was. This was the reason that I had never attempted to search for him. It was only in silence. In silence I used to search for him in any happy or difficult moments. All the time the same question: Where are you, my star? My eyes were searching through endless space until they stopped at the most beautiful and most shining star. There you are! I found you. And using my hand I sent a kiss to you. And I did this quite often. I knew how to do it. I was used to it. But now? What shall I do?

Stupid! I answered myself. You will do nothing.

My sister came back to the room and asked, "Would you like to see him?"

"Are you really that crazy? How can I do that?" I answered in anger.

"Okay, as you like it," she said and left again.

Arbi! Mixed feelings again. Powerful emotions! I wanted to see him. Wanted to talk to him. Wanted.... what? What did I want?! The desire, my beautiful dream. I wanted to touch it with my own hand. But is this possible? How is it possible that I can do it? There was a war of feelings within me... Now I already knew my position. I was mother to a grown up son. Was it right to think about myself, for myself now at this age? What if my son would feel ashamed of me? I went to my sister and told her what I was thinking. She looked up to the sky and spoke, "Great God! But you, what, eh? What desire do you have? Wow, how suppressed you are! Who really am I dealing with? Do whatever you want!"

Now my calmness was gone. What did she want by telling me that? Every passing hour my desire to see Arbi was increasing. But I didn't dare. In the midst of this turmoil of thoughts I decided to go to the beach for a week. Maybe there I would recover from this turmoil and return calm again. I expressed this idea to my son.

"Okay! At the beach or here, I find it the same," he said. "The beach is only one hour from here. It is easy for me to come with you and return whenever I want."

I embraced him for understanding. He turned to me and asked, "Are you sure that you are not running away from something? It seems to me that you want to avoid some kind of confrontation."

"What?" He knew me too well. "No, nothing. I simply want to have some relaxation." I tried to avoid his eyes.

"Okay!" He laughed. "I can come and meet the village girls whenever I want."

He did not hesitate to tell me what he felt. But me, why was I so ashamed to talk honestly with him? I could not explain it. Maybe all mothers feel it difficult to express thoughts about themselves...

Next day we left for the beach. I brought with me all those mixed feelings. Though so many years had passed, the wound in my heart was badly exacerbated. Wow! How strange are we human beings! We keep within ourselves one special dream. This dream keeps the fire burning all through life. The most important dream to us! Love! How strange! How true!

I was silent all the way, gazing through the window at those relaxing views of the village. I felt lost in that space. I was searching for something with my mind's eye.

Where are you, my star?

My eyes are lost in space
covered by the longing tears
and my lips burning of a kiss
are in search of those lips!

Years are gone, melted away
just like this open space
in me feelings still survive
with desire for that kiss!

My eyes close, tears run
and my heart invites the joy
lips tremble in deep yearning

where are you, my star?

I was looking rather surprised through the window of my bedroom. Wow! It truly was beautiful. My son was playing by the shore with a girl I had never seen before. She looked very beautiful! I was hearing their true and sincere laughs. My son was tall and brown skinned. I often used to talk to myself while looking at him. He is very handsome. Still inside me I knew that every mother thinks the same way of her son or daughter. I used to find it hard to think of a girl that would indeed match the quality of my son. However, this girl did attract my attention. Tall, beautiful and full of vitality. Her long legs gave her a true elegance. Though playing barefoot, they looked very comfortable in the dense sand of the beach.

For a moment, I sensed a feeling of being left out. He had not told me anything about such a beautiful girl and his friendly relations with her. Maybe boys don't express themselves so much. They are more straightforward in actions. However, I was rather satisfied with what I was seeing now. I was not going to disturb them. I'd leave them in peace and let them decide when they want to come inside for breakfast. Instead I was going back to my soft and comfortable bed and doze a little.

Oooh, what a good feeling! I took a deep breath, closed my eyes and continued to enjoy that quiet moment. The soft sheets were fondling my body, giving me more relaxation. My eyes became heavier. It did not take long time before I heard a whispering in my ears.

"Greetings!"

- What? What! Who, when? I was murmuring confused words and was trying to push words out of my mouth. That voice was very familiar and dear to me.

"Come closer! Why do you stay so far away?"

I rubbed my eyes forcibly. Tried to speak again.

"You are here?! Who told you? How did you come here?! I can't believe it, indeed!" But my words still seemed garbled. Whatever I tried, I only could murmur. I looked at him surprised and kept talking. "I have never had the courage to search for you. How is it possible that you are here?"

His familiar smile made me stop talking.

"Come close to me!" And he embraced me with all his strength. His eyes were penetrating deep into mine. His breathing so close to my mouth.

"True that you have not searched for me, but you have never forced me out of your mind. Isn't it so?" he asked looking again deep into my eyes. His hot breathing was speeding up. "I am very sure about what I am saying."

It was true. He was with me in every moment of my life. In my mind and heart. Oh, how long had that feeling remained within me! And here it is now, just a tiny sparkle and everything seems as if it happened yesterday.

"Why are you so sure?" I said to provoke him.

"Because I know you very well. You are that other half of me. This will never change."

I was left open-mouthed. Words got stuck in my throat. Everything he was saying was true. And it didn't end here. His warm breath, his caressing invaded my whole being, just like a soft, warm blanket that I would never wish to remove. Ah! How much I was in need of that warmth! I breathed deep while enjoying the whisperings coming out of his lips. His words were like a beautiful and loveable melody to my ears.

"Tell me about yourself. What has happened with you during all this time?" I asked him in awe.

"What shall I tell you? I have not much to tell. I never married. I never could replace you with somebody else. Here I am now just as you see me. A bachelor in love for my whole life with the same girl."

"You are crazy!" I told him. "It's not fair that you should stay so long without a lover. You know that I got married. Why should you stay like this?"

"I tried, but I couldn't." His answer was sharp as if to say---enough now, I don't want to talk about this topic. "You tell me now about yourself." He shook me and hugged me again.

I started to tell him everything from the beginning up to those moments.

"I have learned a lot of things in America. Life there was indeed a new schooling, but difficult and beautiful, too. Difficult because everything is a beginning. The language, the way of living, the rules. But on the other end, it's beautiful because you grow yourself as a person, as a female. Besides that, there are a lot of opportunities there."

I told him how the American women are everywhere and in every field of life: doctors, businesswomen, politicians and more. Everywhere they have equal rights. "But when will this happen here for us, tell me, when? Why shouldn't we here say STOP to the violence against women, huh?"

His eyes looked like they were throwing sparkles of joy. So it seemed to me, at least. His powerful arms pulled me close to his body.

"Change begins with yourself," he answered lightly and easily.

His words were so close to my ear: my best, my strongest, my dearest!

Again that beautiful melody in my ears. Again encompassed by that so warm and composed melody full of sweet words of love. Caressing, whispering, melody. Again, again and again. Hot breathing that passed from one lip to the other. That warm blanket had now surrounded our two bodies as if one single body. All around me in that room endless colors were forming a rainbow. That so beautiful melody was now being sung by both of us. The colors seemed to melt together with that melody. A sweet feeling kept exploding within the circle of that rainbow which encircled our bodies. It was impossible to avoid it. That magic feeling was so sweet and hid a volcanic explosion that would cover everything in its way. We both had now already turned into a mutual volcano. And the volcano received added strength from each kiss and each hug. Now and then I would see fireworks exploding in the air. It was a miracle! I did not want this moment ever to end. I began to speak, "I don't want, no I don't want this moment to ever end. Never! Never." I tried to raise my voice.

Arbi heard me and said, "Why must it end? It is your dream. It is in your hand. Do you hear me? It is in your hand."

His voice was clear and clean. Later on it trailed off leaving behind the strange echo: Youuuuu haaaave it iiin youuuuur haaaand!

No, nooo! Please do not leave. Why must you leave? No, don't! I tried to shout, but my voice got stuck in my throat. I started to poke with my hands here and there around me in that beautiful dream. Tried to open my eyes. In the beginning I could not see clearly in that murky moment. Later the view became clearer.

- What? Simply a dream? Unbelievable! But I wondered, why did it seem so true? I tried to bring back once again in front of my eyes those endless fragments of conversation and those caressings and kisses. How awful! Only a dream. It was so beautiful. I was clearing up my mind now. To my surprise, in my mind, more than anything else, remained that echo of his voice:

"You have it in your hand," I spoke to myself. The same echo in my head again : Youuu haaave it iiin youuur haaand! It iis youuur dreeaam.

It's useless what you are saying! That's nonsense. I started this dialogue with myself. Why! Who am I that I can hold the dream in my hands? I am a woman who knows only to work twelve hours a day to meet the demands of the family. This much did I know to do. As soon as I raised my voice for something unjust, that voice would be nipped in the bud. My desires and passions were so suppressed that even the fear of dreams would scare me to the bone. What if somebody had heard me now? My whole body now displayed a color that looked like I had just climbed out of a hot tub. My cheeks were burning. I went to the bathroom to see myself in the mirror. I freshened up with cold water in an attempt to come back to myself. I raised my head to see my cheeks. They were still red and burning. I started to talk to the mirror: "Do you see how weak you are?" "You are even scared by a dream. Do you understand now how suppressed you are? You are afraid to explain a dream. I was talking to myself angrily, and I threw my towel at the mirror. It was clear why. I was not able to receive an answer from the mirror (that is from myself). The female inside that mirror was telling the truth. I, indeed, had proved to be weak. But why? Actually I was living in a free world and yet feared to express myself freely. Then, what about hundreds and thousands of girls that don't have the opportunity to move to the Western world? How do they survive? No, I must do something that the dream told me. Change begins with yourself. Yes, very true. I should have changed. I should have been free to express all my desires and dreams. Without being free myself, both psychologically and physically, I would never be able to help anybody else.

I was listening to the news every day, and every day I learned in those news about the violence inflicted on girls and women. And it must be stressed that now a kind of revolution had already started by the youth to fight against the pressure and violence on women. Still much work needed to be done. In the north of the country young girls were victims of violence. Here and there you would hear: father killed his daughter because she was pregnant by her lover. Or a husband killed his wife because she had requested a divorce. This was still a big wound on our society. Why didn't I become part of that society that was fighting against old customs and habits that kept the female so subdued ? Why?

- It is youuur dreeaam .... youuu haaave iiit in youuur haaand.

The echo of those words drove powerfully back into my head. Yes, I smiled. It is true. I must raise my voice. Must win my freedom. Without doing this for myself, how can I help others? My eyes were clear now. Clouds were floating away from my brain and everything was clear and clean. The smile returned to my face. Yes, it would be very beautiful. I took a deep breath and tried to look as normal as I could. I don't know if it came from the monologue with myself or from the dream I had seen minutes ago.

The fresh air coming through my room's window filled my lungs with oxygen. I heard the noise when the main door was opened.

"Mom!" called my son. "It's almost ten o'clock a.m. You are not up yet? Come on, please! I am so hungry. What has happened to you today? You have never slept so late."

His voice was echoing all through that small house by the sea.

"Mom," he called again, come down , please, because I want to present to you a beautiful girl. It has been for a long time that you've been telling me find a girl, find a girl and start a relationship with her. And here she is now!"

"Coming, I am coming," I said, surprised for having slept so much.

I came down to the kitchen touching my cheeks with my hands. How did I look first thing in the morning?. Oh-oh! Oh boy! How shall I explain this situation? I tried to appear calm.

"Come, Mom! This is my friend, Ana." My son was so joyous. And the girl named Ana showed a sweet smile. I embraced her slightly, saying, "I am glad to meet you!"

It was a little late for the breakfast omelettes, but both wanted to eat. They kept looking at each other straight in the eyes, whispering and laughing. How straightforward and frank they seemed! It was beautiful, indeed, to see them like two little birds chirping, full of joy. While eating breakfast I felt that my son was observing me now and then.

"What's happened with you?" he said. "You never sleep so late? Are you okay? You look a bit pink in the face. Maybe you have some fever?"

"No, no," I spoke decisively but scared as well because of the dream that just flashed back into my mind. "I wanted to stay a little longer in bed but then I fell asleep again. Nothing else," I answered as if guilty.

"You are hiding something from me," he said.

"Enough with this silliness!" I answered quickly." Come on now. Tell me how did you two meet each other."

My boy looked at the girl as if to tell her 'it is your turn first.' She smiled and started to tell, "In the beginning it was a physical attraction. After that we began to know each other better until a moment came when he," and she pointed to the boy, "invited me to the first meeting. I was happy because this was a real date, but I did not give in at first. I told him: 'I don't date boys who smoke.'" While talking she was laughing very sincerely. "And he did not hesitate. He looked at the cigarette, looked at me, and then threw the cigarette away. This gesture made me laugh loudly and it seemed to me very romantic. After several dates and having had some time with each other, we became very close and now we feel good together. That is all," she finished and looked at the boy. He rustled her hair with his hand and kissed her lightly on the forehead.

"It's very interesting how you got to know each other. I wish you a long and beautiful relationship." I embraced them both and went to clean the things in the kitchen. But again I plunged into deep thought. Finally my son came to me and said,

"You seem completely lost ! What is happening with you? I mean it seriously? Have we come here for a vacation or not? Come on, loosen up. Laugh a little now!"

"You're right, son. I'm sorry! I have done nothing with you. On the contrary, I feel very glad, indeed, when I see you two so joyful. You know how much I have suffered myself. Therefore I don't even have the smallest prejudice."

"I know, Mom, I know it," he said. "But that time is gone. Now you enjoy seeing your son who has no prejudices whatsoever."

"Yes." I smiled and kissed him on the forehead. "You have done much right. I am very happy for you. You just go and have a shower now, and I am going to have a walk along the shore."

The pair were glad that they would be alone together again, and ran up the stairs teasing each other. Even when they were already upstairs, I could still hear their cheerful laughing and kisses.

"Go into the room!" I shouted just to joke with them. They both laughed.

I went outside bearing within me a great joy for my son, but yet confused in my mind after the dream I had seen. While walking silently by the shore it appeared to me as if life really was that easy. All around me I could see a perfect combination nature had put together. But looking up through the horizon the view seemed complicated. Sea, sand, bare feet. Here and there clouds that looked like a white veil, and some other darker ones which seemed as if they were chasing the sun. But their attempts were useless because the sun rays appeared again and again, shining over everything around.

Once more that echo coming from the dream was back in my head: It iis iin youuur haaand. It iis youuur dreeeaaam....

My long and curly hair, brushed by the sea breeze, was flying from one side of my head to the other. How strange are we human beings? Just as our locks are blown about by the winds, so our own thoughts become entangled in our minds. My hands nervously kept pushing and tossing my hair on either side as if to find an answer... It iis youur dreeaaam... this statement was again sstriking like a hammer in my head. Am I right? I still wonder. Do I have the right to think about my dreams now that my son is grown? Oh, God! How limited my thoughts had become! The past and the violence exercised on me in that past had left such strong mental consequences that now, I myself, was judging whether it is right or wrong to think about a beautiful dream.

I spoke to myself again. "Hey, stupid you! Pull yourself together."

No, no. I have no reason to keep my silence anymore. I will even take the courage and search for other dreams that have been left deep, deep in the drawer.

I raised my eyes upward to look at the horizon and took a deep breath. Far there up on the horizon a gigantic bird was gliding up and down very quickly. First down , touching the top of the hill, and then again whirling up to the sky. How magnificent it looked! For a moment it seemed to me that my dreams, too, were flying in the same direction that the free bird was flying. Fly eagle! Keep flying that way with grandeur--proud and free!

The light breeze by the seashore made you feel completely different from the real world. You felt yourself privileged to enjoy the spiritual tranquility that the sea, the sand, and the bare feet gave you. Very pleased, I rubbed my eyes. Am I still in the dream? I laughed to myself. No, I was not in the dream. I started to run quite lightly, lightly.

"Eeemmaaa! Eeemmaaa!"

"Who called me? Was it a fake echo in my ears?"

"Emma, it is me! Wait for me."

My heart started to beat forcefully. It was that same voice so dear to me! The same voice as in the dream!

- "Arbi!" I murmured joyfully. I turned in the direction the voice was coming from.

"What? I was still talking to myself totally shocked. My eyes were wide. My mouth was half-open. And my arms, surprisingly, were spread. My lips were trembling while trying to whisper a soft call: "Where are you, my Star?"

The End